Sweet Temptations:
The Trilogy

L.M. Mountford

L.M. Mountford
United Kingdom
Sweet Temptations
The Trilogy

Publisher's Note: This is a work of fiction. Names, characters, places, and incidents are a product of the author's imagination. Locales and public names are sometimes used for atmospheric purposes. Any resemblance to actual people, living or dead, or to businesses, companies, events, institutions, or locales is completely coincidental.

Edited by readabit: Copy Editing and Proofreading Services Est 2018
L.M. Mountford – 1st Ed.
ISBN: 978-1-913945-98-5

Sweet Temptations:
THE TRILOGY

THE LORD OF LUST
L.M. MOUNTFORD

Sweet Temptations:

THE BABYSITTER

THE LORD OF LUST

L.M. MOUNTFORD

Sweet Temptations:
The Babysitter

L.M. MOUNTFORD

Chapter One

Richard Martin always hated Holmes & Raine's Christmas parties. The décor reminded him of a cheap Hammer Horror set. The atmosphere was reminiscent of a funeral. And worst of all, they were organised in August and hosted in early November.

Each year, the bosses would present a laundry list of reasons for the premature celebration, but everyone knew those were merely a smokescreen, devised to mask the fact that it cost considerably less to hold a Christmas party before December. Frankly, Richard wondered why they bothered even holding a party, or, for that matter, made attendance mandatory.

Subtly pushing up his left sleeve cuff, he checked his watch for what felt like the hundredth time. To his utter disgust, the digital display indicated that it was just *10:03 pm*. The *party* would go on for at least another hour, maybe even two, God forbid!

The dining hall of the Cheltenham Premier Inn was a hive of colour and light as the *value* disco ball fitted to the ceiling pelted the chamber with light beams and the speakers blared out a stream of Christmas hits from the 90s. The walls were decorated in red and white. Mistletoe hung on strands of crimson silk, and an artificial Christmas tree stood in the centre of the room beside a folding table heavily laden with snacks and refreshments. The guests appeared jubilant and festive as they revelled in small groups evenly spaced around the cavernous chamber, mirroring the groups that clung together around the office's coffee and tea machines. They were garbed elegantly in suits and dresses, a façade of wealth and importance that was as phoney as their smiling faces. God, he needed a drink.

Resisting the urge to check his watch, Richard got up from his assigned seat and moved into the crowd, the wooden soles of his shoes clapping loudly on the tiles as he weaved a path between the mingling bodies, nodding politely at anyone who noticed him, towards the overloaded folding table. There were ample snacks and refreshments, Asda's finest. Diced sausage rolls, cocktail sausages, crisps, biscuits, fruit and cheese on cocktail sticks, mini-pizzas, and even some slices of chocolate sponge, all laid out in white china bowls and saucers around two large bottles of Jacob's Creek and Honeyed Jack Daniel's, as well as a jug of iced orange squash. Two high towers of Styrofoam cups had been erected between the bottles.

Taking the cup on the top of the tower, he contemplated the wine for a moment, tempted to pour a drink, but then thought better of it. Alice would kill him if she found out. Grumbling inwardly, he mournfully poured himself a squash. The wine was probably vinegar anyway, he reasoned, before twisting to take another look around the room while sipping the fruity beverage.

He glimpsed Stacy Stevens, a pretty part-timer, in the firm's mailroom with long raven black hair and milky skin, nervously edging through the crowd in her black lacy dress and flat-bottomed shoes; somehow seeming even more uncomfortable than him amongst the revellers. Nearby, he saw Mark McClaine, his office colleague and friend, and his wife Rachael deep in conversation with another couple he didn't recognise. And deepest amidst the denizens, the firm's MD, Derik Holmes, was conversing with the heads of departments and grinning broadly as he took long swigs from a monogrammed silver and crocodile-leather hip flask. Silver-haired, rosy-faced, and with the frame of a barrel wrapped in Armani, Derik was the very embodiment of opulent living and Richard could only hope the man didn't notice him for he was awfully fond of mocking and belittling anyone whom he considered beneath him. Fortunately, the four department heads seemed to be commanding the full wrath of the Director's humour and he failed to notice the lowly bookkeeper standing beside the refreshments. Alas, there was no sign of Alice amidst the sea of faces, but neither, thankfully, could he see…

"Well, well, well, look who we have here?" an all too familiar voice said silkily.

Fuck. Throwing his head back, Richard drained the cup in a single swig before placing it back on the table and turning, slowly, around to be confronted by the vision of his supervisor, Scarlet Holmes, standing before him. Strikingly beautiful with soft features and sun-kissed skin, her hair was long, wavy tresses of honey blonde that reached down to her shoulders. Clad in a dark blue pencil dress that went well with her almost unnaturally bright baby blue eyes and clung to her slender figure, the low-cut V-neckline offering a tantalising glimpse of her ample cleavage, she would have seemed utterly radiant if he hadn't known the beauty was only skin deep.

"Hi Scarlet," he said nervously before flashing her a smile he was certain Stevie Wonder would have seen through; "enjoying the party?"

"Mmm…" she purred, watching him with a wicked amusement that Richard wasn't sure he liked. Then again, he rarely knew how to feel around Scarlet Holmes. Though she'd only been twenty-three and barely out of University when she joined the firm, she was also the CEO's daughter and had leapt over the heads of a dozen more highly qualified employees to get the Accounting Supervisor's position. What made it all the worse was, unlike the stereotypical cliché of a ditzy boss's daughter, Scarlet actually knew her trade. Despite having an attitude that constantly swung from aggressive to flirtatious, she had a genuine business acumen as well as a knack for people and figures. She was ambitious and worked tirelessly to ensure that she and her people regularly went above and beyond. Thanks largely to her efforts, they were now the top performing team in the firm and rumour had it, she was about to be promoted to the Head of the Accounts Department. However, there were also whispers. Rumour had it that she'd had numerous affairs with more than half the firm's employees, many of whom were happily married. For his part, Richard preferred not to put stock in the storm of office gossip that followed where ever she went, but in one thing, at least, the rumours were true. She was a real tight arse.

"Where's your wife? I haven't seen her. Is everything alright between you two?"

"Oh…" His eyes flickered towards the door leading out of the hall to the building's main foyer, hoping against hope to see his wife sashaying towards them. "Alice just stepped out for a minute. She had to take a call but couldn't hear herself over the music." His tongue darted out to moisten his dry lips. "She should be back any minute now." And he hoped that was true. The words sounded hollow to his ears, sounding foreign and unfamiliar and he suddenly had the feeling of being trapped as he realised just how close they were, her curvaceous body all but pinning him against the table. "So-so, how's your father? He looks like he's…enjoying himself."

He gestured with a nod over her shoulder and Scarlet twisted to a look back across the hall to where her father was telling a very animated story. At the sight of a short and portly man with thinning red-grey hair Richard had seen around the office a few times but had never been introduced to, standing a few paces away, she made only a token effort to cover her laugh with a cough. With a face such a deep shade of red it was almost purple and watching the inside of his cup so intently, clearly determined to look anywhere but at his immediate superior, the tomfoolery could only have been at his expense.

"Well, you know Daddy, always happy so long as there is a drink in his glass and minions to torment." It was meant as a joke and Richard tried to match her gleeful chuckle, but his heart just wasn't in it and he could tell she saw through the façade. Suddenly, her playfulness evaporated.

When she turned back, the stern mask that so often watched him like a hawk whenever he handed in his reports suddenly glared up at him with eyes as cold and hard as diamonds. The shift was so abrupt it almost gave him vertigo. "He has his eye on you."

"Me?" Swallowing the knot suddenly rising in his throat, he forced himself to hold her gaze, fighting the impulse to glance towards the Director. The urge was like burning fishing lures hooked into his eyes, tugging insistently, and he fully expected to spy the Managing Director shooting him a glare, the mirror image of his daughter's. But why? What the hell would walrus face want with him?

"The Prometheus Account." Scarlet supplied by way of explanation, arching one perfectly plucked eyebrow. Full pink lips pulled tight into an almost indefinable line.

Prometheus was a London based construction and land developments company that had several branches throughout the continent and, according to their books, also had contracts in parts of Central America, Asia, Africa and the Middle East. Though it was not exactly an uncommon practice for big organisations to outsource their accounts, indeed Holmes & Raine had more than a dozen such contracts, there was no question that the Prometheus Account was a big deal. Rumour had it that Derik Holmes had superseded two department heads to ensure his daughter received the account. With explicit instructions, it was to be given top priority. Whether that was true or not, she, in turn, had called Richard into her office and instructed him to delegate his workload around the rest of the team. She wanted Prometheus to be his sole concern. Everything else was to go on the back burner. So he had.

She'd also told him to have it done ASAP. That had been three weeks ago, and the reports were still stashed on the flash drive he kept locked away in his desk drawer.

"Ahhh..." He swallowed, the knot in his stomach leaping sickeningly into his throat. He should have known. Hell, he should have given her the damn USB last week. Withholding it had been stupid.

For all the weight laid on his shoulders, it hadn't taken him long at all to sort and organise and check Prometheus' accounts. It was such easy work; a trained chimp would have been up to the task. Their records were meticulous and immaculate. The numbers perfect. And, what with the pressure to finish the job, the importance of the contract to the company and the fact his performance review was upcoming; withholding the data was more trouble than his job's worth. Withholding it had been very stupid, but Richard couldn't help himself. In his twelve years in accounting, he had never seen anything like it, and that irked him. He couldn't put his finger on what, the numbers were just...too perfect. Or too perfect to be genuine.

Of course, it wasn't any concern of his. He wasn't an analyst. It wasn't his job to sort out conundrums. He just kept the client's books. When he was done, he sent reports to Scarlet with notes about his concerns and recommendations, if any; but in this, he couldn't help himself.

It almost felt like there was a challenge hidden amidst the sheer mass of paper and data, of piles of receipts, invoices and spreadsheets. Something secret only he could see. Hidden, waiting, daring him to find it. So, he'd begun to dig, looking deeper, trying to solve a mystery that common sense screamed didn't exist, but that the small voice in the back of his mind refused to let go, like some naughty schoolboy playing truant to go on a great adventure in the land of Narnia.

Sooner or later though, the boy needed to go back through the wardrobe, and if the Managing Director had his eye on Richard... So far, every money trail had turned up empty and by itself, mere professional curiosity wasn't worth losing a job over. Or, worse still, becoming the next punchline in one of walrus face's jokes.

Baleful blue eyes glared up at him, chunks of blue ice burning bright against a sea of soft beauty. Richard forced a small, reassuring smile. "I'll have them on your desk Monday.

"Good" That single word was like a storm passing to unveil sunbursts. She beamed with the radiance, her golden skin lighting up with a warmth that chased any hint of chill away as those luscious pink lips curled into a smile. "See that you do, or else I might just have to give you a spanking." She winked.

Richard gawped, not sure whether to believe his own ears. Had she really just said that?

To anyone who might have glanced their way, the gesture would have appeared innocent. Yet her eyes lost none of their intensity as she watched him, and her playful tone sent a warm, involuntary shiver coursing up his spine. What the fuck?

He remembered all the stories he'd heard people at work gossiping about the people who'd told them and the wide range of vague, outlandish details that seemed to grow more and more extraordinary with each retelling. It was all hearsay. Mostly just the petty vindictiveness of someone who'd been put out, or thought her job should have been theirs, or just the usual rambling talk that always seemed to blossom around a famous name. There had never been any proof, and until now, Richard had barely given them much thought. But that look in her eyes made him ready to believe every word. He'd seen it on the cats he sometimes saw stalking city streets on his morning drive to work. There was the same confidence, the same purpose and... hunger.

She watched him the way a stalking cat would observe a bird pecking in the mud, utterly fixed in its own world and ripe for the plucking, and the thought had him instinctively averting his gaze. Whatever this game was, he didn't want a part of it. However, knowing she was waiting for him to say something, he opened his mouth to agree but the words that should have come caught in his throat and all he could do was nod in acknowledgement. Heat blossoming across his cheeks, he swallowed, his mouth so dry it felt like forcing down a lemon. Goddamnit, he needed a drink.

Her eyes flashed, victorious fire dancing over cool blue ice. Then, as if only just realising she was making him uncomfortable, her smile faltered for a moment and turned apologetic. "Awww don't worry, Dick. I was only kidding," she cooed like he was a small child or pet dog. "I think you better have another drink. If your face gets any redder, they might mistake you for Rudolph and hang you on the wall." She giggled, the sound all girlish and mocking. "It's already a rather striking likeness. Maybe with a pair of antlers-"

More relieved than embarrassed by her dismissal, Richard turned back to the refreshments before Scarlet had finished speaking. With the Styrofoam cup still in hand and grateful for some much-needed space between him and the teasing wench, he reached out for the jug of squash. To his horror, the hand was shaking. No! God, get a grip man. Don't let her get to you.

As if she knew his thoughts, Scarlet stepped in close enough for him to inhale her perfume. Something sharp and expensive.

"Here, let me," she offered. Brushing his hand aside, she seized the handle and, despite it being almost full, raised the jug one-handed. With a slight pivot of her hips to face him, she filled his cup almost all the way to the top, her gaze unwavering, boring into his with that look of predatory glee, seeing through him, into him. It was unnervingly similar to the look Alice shot him whenever she suspected he was up to something. "There." She put the jug down before finally breaking the contact to give the drink a quizzical look. "Just orange? You don't want to mix it with something a little stronger?"

"N-no thanks. I'm driving." Barely able to get his tongue around the words, Richard had to fight the urge to immediately knock the drink back. Fuck, where the hell was Alice? What could Samantha have to say that couldn't wait for tomorrow? He looked down at the orange in his cup, wished, though he'd never been much of a drinker, that it could be something fermented, and added under his breath without thinking, "Alice would kick my arse if she found out I'd been drinking." The moment he'd said them, he regretted the words. Beaten, he surrendered and chucked the juice back in almost one big gulp. It was deliciously refreshing and eased the knots in his gut in a single rush of watered citrus.

"Ohhh…" Mirth lit up Scarlet's eyes. "Well, isn't someone a slave driver. Come on, Dick, I promise I won't tell…" she teased, playfully reaching for the Honeyed Jack Daniel's. Richard struggled not to grin at the impish mischief on her face.

"No, it's fine, I don't really like mixing drinks anyway."

She feigned a pout that had no doubt melted her daddy's heart more than once. It had the effect of making her look so serenely demure and girlish. He might have been convinced she was sincere if not for that wild glint in her eyes. It was a sinful look on her, the perfect melding of innocent and wicked. All that was missing was an Anne Summers costume, probably a nurse or cheerleader's uniform.

A shiver coursed up at his spine at the thought of Scarlet in such a skimpy ensemble. Her long legs encased in knee socks and vanishing into a miniskirt that seemed to promise a glimpse of whatever she had on, or not, underneath with every movement. A tight-fitting crop top stretched tight over her full breasts but cut just short enough to show off her flat stomach. Golden hair bouncing in pigtails as she played with a set of pom-poms…

Richard mentally shook himself, trying to clear the image. He wasn't a horny teen anymore. Those sorts of thoughts were trouble. He was married. And she was his boss. Off limits didn't even begin to cover it. However, his body apparently disagreed and, to his horror, the image roused a very vital part of his anatomy into life. Registering the stirring, he instinctively glanced down to see an already visible bulge rising against his left trouser leg. He shifted, trying to cover his visibly straining erection before glancing back up. But Scarlet must have already noticed because the pouting girl was gone. Instead, she was grinning toothily, her eyes bright. Pink tongue darting out to slowly moisten her full kissable lips, she mouthed "busted."

Time held its breath. Somewhere in the hall, a guffaw rang out. The timing was purely coincidental, but even still the humiliation hit him like a bucket of ice water. Dammit, what the fuck was going on? He couldn't believe this was happening. He needed to think, to get some air before this got any worse and his boss decided to whip out her phone to immortalise the moment.

Contrary to being impeded, however, the realisation he'd been caught only had Richard's cock stiffening to full mast against its confinement. To his enormous relief, no one else appeared to notice.

Scarlet's eyes widened, her smile faltering to form a perfect 'O'. "Oh… my!"

Well-aware of what had caught her attention, Richard turned his eyes up to the hall's plain white ceiling and ornamental brass chandelier-style lights draped with tinsel, desperate to look at something, anything, but the woman eyeing his dick. To his enormous relief, no one else appeared to have noticed. He felt like a little Robin red breast that had spotted a cat stalking it in the grass and taken flight, rising high on a wing of elation and the adrenaline of escaping death. Only to be swatted from the sky and brought crashing back down, its last moment consumed by the image of the sleek feline body arching into the sky, hooked claws reaching out and fangs bared. I tawt I taw a puddy tat, indeed.

"Have you heard anything about your promotion?" he asked without thinking, studying the interlaced webs of gold, red and green tinsel that enveloped the nearest light.

"Y-yes…" For all her customary swagger, the silky soft voice sounded breathless and the shaky timbre drew his gaze irresistibly back to her. Scarlet glared back at him. Her eyes narrowed and cheeks tinged a faint shade of pink. She seemed to be musing about whether to say more, searching for a trap behind the question, and the uncertainty reflected in those bright blue irises had him blowing out a slow breath that released all the tension from his body.

Scarlet obviously sensed, or noticed, the change in him, however, because the gleam of predatory amusement returned to her eyes. She'd play whatever game he had in mind, and she'd play to win. "Daddy says the job's mine if I want it, but first I need to get my house in order. He's starting to think we might have a loose cannon on deck." She leant casually back against the refreshments table with her hands gripping the edges to distribute her weight and back, curving just enough to emphasise her breasts. It was a pose that would have put many magazine centrefolds to shame. "But let's not talk shop. This is a party, after all. How is your son, Alex, isn't it? I saw the pictures on your desk. He must be nearly two now?"

Richard held her gaze, refusing to take the bait even as his eyes were instinctively drawn to the slopes of her breasts. "Almost sixteen months, yes." He swallowed, a bitter taste rising in the back of his throat, not liking the way this conversation was turning. "And he's fine, hasn't quite got the hang of walking yet. Can't quite find his feet, so he's always losing his balance mid-step. We've had a lot of scuffs and tears, but he keeps getting back up." He couldn't quite keep the pride from his voice. So many kids would burst into a fit of tears whenever they fell over and refuse to move until their parents picked them up, but Alex never stopped. Even in tears, he would push himself up and keep crawling to where he wanted to go.

"And you and Alice are coping well?" she asked, cocking her head to the side. A curl of locks fell out of place, but Scarlet didn't brush it aside, her eyes searching his. "I doubt it could have been easy starting a family so soon after losing your job. Your career taking such a huge step back and having to pack up your lives to move here. Not many marriages could weather the storm so well. Maybe you two should write one of those self-help books. Money woes and job lows - A couple's survival guide." She chuckled, the sound dry and mocking.

Forcing a small smile, Richard resisted the impulse to give her the finger. *I prefer Don't Let the Tarts Get You Down.* "We're Fine." Of course, it was a half-truth. They fought, sometimes like cats and dogs, over nothing at all, and other times they fought to avoid the very real issues looming over them. There had been many of those recently, but he wasn't about to discuss that with Scarlet.

"I see." With that, she pushed away from the table and fingered the stray lock of hair back behind her ear. "Tell me, Dick, would you consider it cheating to kiss me under the mistletoe?" She said it casually, as if it was as every day as asking about the weather.

Already on edge and walking on eggshells, the broadside caught Richard completely by surprise and had him almost doubling over in a fit of dry, heaving coughs so violent it was a marvel he didn't choke. "Ex-ex-excuse me?" he stammered, certain he must have misheard her.

Smiling teasingly, she stepped closer so that as she looked up; they were almost nose-to-nose. "It was a perfectly simple question." A hand tipped by baby blue nails reached out, taking the cup from his grasp and placing it on the refreshment table before tracing her finger up along the lapel of his jacket and along the line of his jaw. "Would you consider kissing another woman under the mistletoe as being unfaithful to your wife?"

Her eyes flickered to the ceiling overhead and, pressing firmly on his chin, she tilted his head back. Too stunned to resist, he followed her gaze skyward to where three leaves of mistletoe were hanging off a scrap of crimson silk dangling above their heads.

Richard's chest constricted. "I…I…"

"Cat got your tongue?"

Richard wheeled, the pit falling out of his stomach as the all too familiar voice asked and brought a frosty blast of reality. Alice Serena Martin stood not three steps away with her arms crossed and glaring at her husband. "Am I interrupting something?" she asked icily.

"Darling," Richard tried to make the greeting sound reassuring, but the rush of fear and arousal the sight of her provoked in him at that moment made it hard to do anything. Even after all the years they'd been married, the sight of her could still leave him speechless. Pale as milk and utterly gorgeous, she wore only the smallest amount of makeup and a sultry, backless evening gown of black satin that moulded perfectly to her hourglass figure. A slit from thigh to hem flashed a glimpse of smooth, flawlessly toned legs that seemed to go forever as she walked. Though shorter than most, her tiny stature barely scraping five feet when propped up by the stilettos she'd worn for the party, his wife was a downright knockout with her sharp, pronounced bone structure, hair that ran down her back in a long wash of silken mahogany, and intense grey-blue eyes.

Yet now her beauty had been contorted into a twisted mask that gave her the hard face of a hawk. Eyes that had stared up at him with such love and devotion, now piercing with accusation. That look cut deeper than steel. He wanted to say something to reassure her, but, somehow, a line like 'it's not what it looks like' just didn't seem it.

"Ahh, Alice!" Scarlet stepped around Richard, into the older woman's sights. She beamed, her eyes alight with wicked delight. "There you are. We were just talking about you."

Alice's cool gaze shifted to the blonde, her lips pursing into a fine line "Indeed."

"In fact, *Dick* was just telling me about your son. He's such a handsome little boy, you must be very proud.

"Yes."

Scarlet gave Richard a slow, appraising look, then smiled knowingly. "He's the spitting image of his father. Good luck keeping the girls away. You'll have to beat them off with a big pole." Dread's cold fingers crept down Richard's spine at Scarlet's added emphasis. Dammit, was she going to try and start a fight?

Though the women had only met on a handful of occasions, exchanging barely more than a handful of words each time, for whatever instinctive, irrational reason, the atmosphere had crackled around them. He could feel it building, raising the hairs on the back of his neck, and knew that rather than finding salvation in his wife, he'd jumped straight out of the frying pan, into the fire.

"Well, I'll manage." Missing nothing, Alice's gaze narrowed momentarily on her husband, who couldn't help shifting guiltily on the balls of his feet under the hawk-like stare, before returning to the younger woman. "But I'm sure you can give me a few pointers sometime. *Dick* tells me you've handled lots of woodwork around the firm." She forced a wry smile. Richard, of course, had never said anything of the sort, but he wasn't about to contradict her. "Your father must be very proud that you're treating his staff so well after he gave you a job?"

For all of a moment, Scarlet's eyes widened in surprise. Then she recovered her composure and her smile melted away into a small, derisive twist. "What can I say? I like to keep the men under me satisfied. Dick's never has any complaints." Alice's nostrils flared and the fingers that had been creeping down Richard's spine closed around his gut, but Scarlet appeared not to notice. She shrugged, her eyes trailing over Alice from head to toe, scrutinising her like she would a document that came across her desk. "That's such a lovely dress, Alice. Is it new?"

Oh, fuck! Richard didn't need to look at his wife to know that, if Scarlet was trying to pick a fight, then she'd just hit her mark. He knew he should step in, but Alice shot a look that warned him to stay out of it. The corner of her lip rose just enough to reveal the glint of white teeth, something she only did when she meant business and had him glancing nervously around the room.

Fortunately, no one seemed interested in taking advantage of the buffet or paying the confrontation any notice, yet.

"You deserve to treat yourself." Scarlet pushed on, her voice laced with a sympathetic tone that was all pity and mocking. "Was it hard to find one in your new size? It would be just awful after you worked so hard to shed the last of that pesky baby weight, but I guess some things just can't be helped..."

Alright, he needed to put an end to this. Whatever Scarlet's game was, she had gone over the line.

Like so many women, Alice had always been overly self-conscious of her appearance. While no one could ever accuse his 110-pound wife, who could put away a whole pizza like Richard did a good 18oz steak, of being anorexic, she was borderline obsessive about her weight. One of her main requirements, when they'd been flat hunting, was that there had to be a nearby gym, and she visited it almost daily. After Alex was born, she'd worked hard to rid herself of the pregnancy pounds and even harder now to maintain her figure. She would give back as good as she got and believed in taking the bull by the horns. If a child tried to fob off not doing their homework, she called them on it. When something went wrong at home and he wasn't in, she dealt with it.

So, if Scarlet wanted a fight, Alice would damn well give her one. Even if that was exactly what the little strumpet was counting on.

Richard opened his mouth to intervene, not at all interested in finding out just what his wife might say, or do for that matter, with so many people around them. Only Scarlet rounded on him before he could get a word out. Her eyes were bright with an impish mischief that made him want to run a hand through his hair.

"Anyway." She cocked her head as if remembering an afterthought, her hair tumbling over one shoulder and exposing the long slope of her neck, as well as giving him a glimpse down the valley of her breasts. "I just so happened to notice that piece of mistletoe hanging up there. So, I asked *Dickie* if he considers it being unfaithful to kiss me." She slid forward a step. Heat bristled across the back of Richard's neck, the fury in Alice's stare burning his skin as Scarlet pressed into him and touched a hand to his cheek before he could think to pull away. The closeness as intoxicating as the perfume suddenly fogging his thoughts and her eyes held his. "It's such a small tradition I know, but they say it's bad luck to ignore it."

"Ohhh really?" Alice shouldered past the younger woman. Scarlet reeled, almost sprawling to the floor, before catching her balance at the last moment. "Then allow me." Her hands tangled in husband's hair, fisting and dragging his head down so their lips crashed together in a fierce kiss.

The sudden embrace stole his breath away and he couldn't help uttering a ragged moan as her tongue forced its way past his lips to meet his in a feverish dance. His hands rose on their own accord to circle around her waist before trailing down her back to grasp her full buttocks, roughly pulling her against him and drawing a low moan from his wife. Then, just as quickly as she had begun, Alice broke the kiss and drew away from the embrace. Short of breath, Richard could only grin down at his wife's satisfied smirk.

"Yea! Get in there, Richard, my son!" Mark called, followed by a sudden uproar of applause and catcalls as every face in the hall zeroed in on them. Breathing hard, Richard forced a smile and raised a hand in thanks, only to be elbowed in the ribs by the equally embarrassed Alice.

"Geez, get a room." Scarlet snarled, her smirk replaced by a scowl. "Maybe you should go before they demand an encore. See you on Monday, *Dick*." Then, starting to worry her bottom lip, she turned on her heel. "Nice to see you again Alice."

"Bitch," Alice cursed under her breath, watching the younger woman's retreating figure with a look of utter malice, before taking her husband's hand in hers and dragging him through the mass of clapping hands and out of the two huge glass doors that opened out onto the Premier Inn's rear garden. It was a cold night, even for mid-November, and the cloudless canopy above twinkled with stars that lit the ground just enough for them to make out the cobbled path leading around the structure to the car park. A frigid wind whistled by and Richard hesitated, remembering that Alice hadn't been wearing a jacket, but she dragged him along. Though wearing five-inch heels, she traversed the tricky stones with ease while he was left almost tumbling over his own feet to keep up with her.

Polished and gleaming, their immaculate black Volkswagen Golf would have been almost invisible in the hotel's car park if not for the solitary lamppost standing sentinel, bathing the vehicle in golden light. Unlocking it with a quick press on the key in his pocket, he held the passenger side door open for his wife to enter the vehicle before closing it and moving around to get in the driver's side. However, no sooner had he pushed the key into the ignition did Alice round on him.

"So, what really happened between you and that tart, Scarlet?" she hissed, seething like a cobra in her venom.

"What? Nothing…. nothing at all…" Richard gasped, shooting her an uneasy smile that he prayed she might find convincing. Her stern look promised otherwise, however, and he quickly turned back to the windscreen, a heavy sigh passing his lips as he fastened his seatbelt and activated the dipped headlights. "Really… it was nothing; she was just asking me a question about mistletoe. And that's all." Twisting the key, he let the engine roar to life and then reversed out of the space before shifting into gear and driving from the car park out onto Gloucester Road.

"Ohhh really…*Dick?*" she spat accusingly, the nickname rolling off her tongue as a long serpentine hiss.

"Ugh! Bloody hell, Alice, this is ridiculous!" he growled, tearing his eyes off the road for a moment to shoot her a reproachful glare. Fortunately, there was little traffic, and the Golf purred like a kitten as they sped along the deserted dual carriageway, angrily challenging every traffic light at a steady 60mph. Yet when a metallic blue Vauxhall convertible roared out of the darkness, overtaking them with a sound like a thunderclap, he couldn't resist the challenge and sped after it. Flooring it, he'd caught up to the sleek two-seater in a matter of seconds, but at a glance from Alice, he eased off the throttle. "Look, I swear, nothing is going on between Scarlet and me."

She watched him suspiciously for a moment more before finally relaxing into her seat, yet he knew she wasn't convinced. Alice was anything but a fool; she'd heard the whispers about his supervisor and, like any good loving wife, she was concerned.

They'd first met fifteen years ago at the University of Bristol. She'd been a 'fresher' studying English literature and out with her *BFFs* on a Saturday night. He'd been a struggling second-year Business Studies student working a double shift in the popular student bar, The Burning Book. While he'd been on the taps, she'd ordered a round of Bloody Marys and when she paid, had handed him a £20 note and a napkin with her mobile number scribbled down. She'd been the first girl to show any real interest in him and, utterly bedazzled by the petite stunner, he'd called her immediately after his shift. Five years later, they were both graduates with promising careers. Alice an English teacher in a prestigious secondary school, him a junior banker. They were also newlyweds, young and in love.

For the first few years of their life as husband and wife, they'd rented a comfortable little flat well within walking distance of Bristol's city centre. However, disaster struck in 2004 when his bank was bought out and amidst the fallout, Richard had lost his job. For the following year they'd lived on a blend of his savings and Alice's salary while he looked for work in the city, but the economic devastation of the recession had left him floundering in a raging river of unemployment and without their prosperous joint income, they'd been forced to move to the smaller, *cheaper*, city of Gloucester.

Feeling the tension hanging between them like a great steel-ball and collar as they left the lights of Cheltenham in their wake and sped down the black stretch of road, Richard changed the subject. "What did Samantha have to say?" Samantha Swift was Alice's oldest and dearest friend, as well as her maid of honour at their wedding. "Shouldn't she be attending to her latest husband's bank balance? Or has the Internet finally run out of shoes and gold?" Alas, the joke fell on deaf ears.

"She's getting divorced."

"What?" He shot her a disbelieving sideways glance. "The ink on her marriage certificate hasn't even dried yet, and she's getting divorced. What happened? Did she bleed the poor bastard dry already? They've only been married a few months."

Growing angry, Alice glared back at him. "No, this time it's different. She caught him in the hot tub with their dog walker." *Damn.*

Feeling his cheeks burn with embarrassment, Richard kept his gaze rooted to the road ahead. Road signs indicated a roundabout half a mile ahead and beyond that, the horizon burned with golden radiance. *Home sweet home.*

Founded at the dawn of the first century AD, on the order of Roman Emperor Nerva and the pride of the Mercian King Æthelred, Gloucester was built along the banks of the River Severn, close to the Welsh border. Though primarily an industrial mecca, the city was a wealth of history and culture, with Tudor architecture still adorning its central streets and the fabled cathedral at its heart.

They drove in silence for several long moments, street lamps bathing them in warm light as they entered the city area. Cruising down Eastern-Avenue past rows of warehouse stores that lined either side, he glimpsed two sets of traffic lights changing from emerald, to amber, to crimson, and began to brake. Downshifting gears, he quickly floored it as the lights changed back just before they came to a complete stop. There were two more sets of lights, but both stayed green as they approached and passed. Despite it being ten-thirty on a Saturday night, the roads were dead and deserted but for the odd cyclist. Houses sprung like weeds as they drove around a roundabout, past a Tesco's garage and took the last exit of an even larger roundabout, capped by a grass isle in its centre. There the road became thin and narrow, winding round numerous snaking twists and flanked with rows of two-storied brick houses on either side, passing a cemetery and an old primary school encircled by high iron spear fencing.

"She's moving into her parents' house on Friday," Alice announced suddenly as they swerved off the main road after passing an ancient church. "I told her you'd be happy to help." She glared at him venomously, as if daring him to refuse.

Steering the vehicle into their parking space, Richard took the car out of gear and put the handbrake on. Taking the key out of the ignition, he turned to his wife, gave her a genuine smile, and said, "Anything for you."

Leaning forward, he seized her lips in a passionate kiss.

Chapter Two

Though the living room door was shut, Richard could dimly hear a movie playing as he shut the front door behind him and Alice. Recognising the cheesy dialogue, he couldn't help but groan in disappointment. *Oh God, please no, not Twilight again!*

The flat was a huge leap down from the one they'd had in Bristol. On the third floor of a five-storey tower block, it had two small bedrooms, one bathroom, and boasted views overlooking Gloucester Park as well as a security door and parking. The rent was also cheap because the flat was on the less desirable side of town.

Slipping off her shoes, Alice went ahead of him and vanished through the wide archway on their right into the kitchen to make a cup of tea whilst he moved down the darkened foyer towards the living room's closed door. "Hey Rebecca, we're home."

A startled gasp and hurried footfalls sounded in answer, and the door was suddenly swung open to reveal a slender feminine figure, shadowed against the bright glare of the living room.

"Hi Mr Martin, sorry, I didn't hear you come in."

"That's okay Rebecca. I know we're back a bit earlier than we said," he assured her, blinking against the sudden flood of light. Fortunately, his eyes adjusted quickly to the blaze, discerning the girl's soft doe-like eyes staring up at him from beneath the smooth wash of dark brown hair that she'd tied into a side braid over her left shoulder. Just nineteen, she had a long, sweet face and a petite yet shapely form that was clad in tight blue jeans and a pink floral T-shirt that ended just above her flat navel. "Has Alex been behaving himself?"

"Oh, he's been just wonderful. Little tyke hasn't made a peep since I put him down." Smiling up at him, she stepped back to let him pass into the flat's living room.

Neither spartan nor lavish, the furnishings were mainly teak and pine, equally as decorative as they were functional, as well as a wide three-person sofa of supple black leather that had been pressed against the wall and a Sony DVD player and 32' television that were mounted on the opposite wall. As he'd feared, the film *Twilight* was playing on the flat screen.

"So, how was the party? Did you have a good time?"

"Boring really. In fact, we were kicked out," he said, barely able to keep the wide grin at bay as he recalled Scarlet's venomous, jilted glare. He would probably pay merry hell for it on Monday, however. Scarlet always loved to play games and Alice had thrown a fine challenge her way tonight.

She may have won the battle, but he was sure the war had only just begun.

Plainly befuddled, Rebecca's eyebrow arched at his comment and for a moment he thought she would press him for further details, but the kettle began to whistle, and he heard Alice shout out a greeting to the girl. As she turned to reply, he took the opportunity to slip past and crossed the room in six quick strides before going through the open doorway leading to the bath and bedrooms. Taking care not to make a sound as he moved down the shadowy antechamber, he crept past the connecting bathroom and master bedroom before coming to the infant's room. Pushing the door ajar, just far enough for him to squeeze through, he stepped cautiously into the gloom beyond. A blue nightlight bathed the interior in a low gloom, illuminating the Star Wars cartoon wallpaper and providing just enough light for him to trek a route around the dozens of toys that lay scattered across the floor.

Sleeping peacefully in his cot, the infant Alexander never stirred as his father approached. If it had not been for his stormy grey-blue eyes and thick dark brown hair, the boy would have been the spitting image of his father and the sight of him curled around his favourite stuffed puppy brought a smile to Richard's face. Given their tenuous financial state, many of their friends and relatives had been surprised by his and Alice's decision to go through with the unexpected pregnancy. But Alice had always wanted to be a mother, and as there was simply no way of telling when the economy would heal, be it ten years or even a hundred. Life was just too short to turn down the blessing life handed them, and they had never been happier since little Alex came into their lives.

Bending forward, he placed a gentle kiss on the child's brow before drawing back and retreating from the room, gently pulling the door shut as he went.

Knowing he should go and pay Rebecca for her help but too eager to get out of his suit, he entered the master bedroom and flicked the light switch before casually shrugging off his jacket. Hurling it across the bed, he'd just begun fingering his tie when there was a sudden knock at the door and he turned around to see Rebecca standing in the doorway, with a sheepish look on her face and her *Twilight* DVD case in hand. Concern stabbed his heart with an icy dagger.

"Hey…Mr Martin, I'm sorry to interrupt you but I'm setting off now and well…my dad's gone away for a couple of days and before he left, he managed to screw up our laptop. I hate to ask, but he'll be home tomorrow and if he comes back to find it broken, he'll just blame me and force me to buy a new one, so…if it's not too much trouble, could you… well um-" The words were spilling from her in a tide of emotion and she looked on the verge of tears.

Richard gave her a reassuring smile. "Of course I can. You go on home and I'll be up to take a look in a minute."

"You will! Oh, thank you Mr Martin; I really appreciate this." Visibly relaxing, she turned on her heel and headed back through to the living room, leaving Richard alone with his thoughts and a quickly mounting temper.

"That rat bastard."

Though they lived on the floor above, he had only met Rebecca's father on one or two occasions, but each had left a lasting impression. Unlike his daughter, Derik Blaire was squat, heavy-shouldered, and prone to violent outbursts. Once happily married and a carrier squaddie, he'd been cashiered after getting drunk and striking an NCO whilst off duty, but still in uniform. A court-martial found him guilty of insubordination, behaviour unbecoming, and wilfully striking a non-commissioned officer. He'd lost his pension and been sentenced to confinement for three years before receiving a dishonourable discharge. In the months after his release, he was dismissed from six occupations before apparently abandoning the search for work. His wife, tired of his bullshit, left him for a younger man and moved up to Yorkshire to escape his continued harassment, leaving their daughter with her growingly aggressive and substance dependent father.

Richard was reluctant to ask about the pair's main source of income. He knew Rebecca worked part-time in a shop over in the Quays, as well as babysitting for them and a few other families in the building. However, that could hardly cover the costs of living, so he was sure there had to be more there than just met the eye.

Loosening his necktie enough to pull it over his head, he hurled the cloth across the bed to join his jacket before starting upon his black shirt but then thought better of it. He and Alice would be going to bed soon enough. There was no point dirtying fresh clothes. Even so, a stab of old vanities caused him to pause before his wife's standing mirror. Tall, clean-shaven, and relatively comely, he had deep blue eyes and medium length raven hair that framed a sharp jaw. Though only thirty-seven, his hair had been salted with a streak of silver, but Alice assured him it made him appear distinguished; he just prayed it didn't foretell his going bald.

Deciding he needed a drink, Richard moved on to the kitchen to find Alice already leaning against the fridge and sipping a steaming cup of tea, waiting for him. A half glass of wine sat on the counter beside her.

"How's Alex?" she asked, setting the cup down on the side and crossing her arms over her waist as he reached for the wine.

"Sleeping peacefully, thank God, and if we're lucky, he'll stay that way till morning. I swear that kid has a set of lungs on him that could wake the dead." Watching her carefully, he brought the glass to his lips and drained it in one swig. It tasted bitter, and he openly shuddered in disgust.

Alice, however, paid no mind to his displeasure. A few stray strands came loose from her thick mane to hang over her eyes, but she brushed them back into place without taking her gaze off him. "So, are you going to help her?"

"Of course I am."

She gave an approving nod. "It's shameful the way he treats her. The sooner she moves out of there, the better." They'd often heard Rebecca talk about moving out, going to live with friends or whatever boy teased her heart. Sometimes she even mentioned renting a little place of her own. However, she never seemed to be able to find enough money and after a few weeks, she'd lose her enthusiasm for the idea until the next time her father lost his temper and threw something at her. "Though I think she will miss you, Richard."

The remark caught him by surprise, and he coughed so hard the wine in his belly almost repeated on him. "Me? I have no idea what you mean, Love."

A sly smile lit up Alice's features and her throaty voice developed a noticeably playful tone. "How could you miss it? She's got a crush on you, Richard," she chuckled. "You're clueless. She watches your every move and smiles whenever she sees you. If she knows you're home, the poor girl gets dolled up just so you'll say she's pretty. And you know, I can't say that I'm not a little jealous." Stepping forward, she took the glass from his hand and placed it on the counter before closing the gap between them, her finger tracing invisible symbols over his chest. "She really is quite beautiful, isn't she?"

Richard's throat ran dry. Was she serious? Was she baiting him, or just stating a fact? Alice had always been blunt, and nobody could deny that Rebecca was certainly very pretty, but how could he agree with her without inadvertently risking her wrath? "Alice, I-"

Her lips silenced him as she suddenly went up onto the tips of her toes, their mouths crashing together in a devouring embrace as her hands moved to encircle his neck. Fierce and demanding, she held nothing back and quickly took the kiss deeper, the passion of it setting a fire in his flesh as her slick tongue invaded the moist warmth of his mouth to meet his own in a feverish dance. He felt his trousers growing tight as his cock sprang to life, powerless to resist his wife's errant ministrations as she drew him against her, one long shapely leg rising, curling around him.

His heart hammered in his chest as he wound his arms around her waist, drawing her closer. Her full breasts pressed against his chest, pebbled nipples poking through the satin like diamonds, and he could feel the heat of her desire against his thigh. His hands, so large upon her tiny frame, trailed down her spine to seize her buttocks, causing her to gasp into the kiss as he pulled her against his hard arousal. It had been so long, he needed her. Now, atop the counter, against the fridge, on the floor, he didn't care. He just had to have her...

"She really is quite beautiful, isn't she?" Her words echoed in his ears, sending a hot shiver down his spine as an image of Rebecca appeared before his eyes. She was arching in pleasure, locked in his arms, whimpering softly as he tasted the hollow of her throat. It was only a momentary lapse, but the mental image was enough to make him jump back, breaking the embrace.

Flushed and breathless, Alice almost lost her balance, and she flashed him an insidious look that both chilled and enflamed his ardour. "What's wrong?"

Fighting to catch his breath, Richard couldn't meet her gaze as guilt's cold fist turned his innards to ice. "We ca-can't do this now. I promised to help Rebecca; her father will be home tomorrow. If I don't go now, it'll be too late."

For a moment she looked as if she were about to protest, but she had always been fond of the girl and after a moment her face softened. She gave a short, defeated nod before turning away. "Fine, just don't be too long."

Her frosty tone was as much a dismissal as a slap in the face, yet as he departed the kitchen, he distinctly heard her declare, "I'll be waiting." The words were rich with promise, and he didn't know whether to cheer or weep.

Chapter Three

He knocked three times and then waited as the sound echoed nine times off the tower's inner walls. The air was thick with the sickly-sweet reek of drugs and somewhere a couple were shouting, their thunderous curses echoing through the walls like clangs on a bell. However, he was too distracted by the painful ache in his groin to take much notice. Digging his hand into his pocket, he tried to relocate his still swollen erection, but the trousers were barely large enough for him to thrust himself down the right leg. The inner pent-up agony persisted, nonetheless.

Shifting uncomfortably, he raised his hand to knock again, only to hear the *click* of the lock's inner mechanics unlocking before the door swung inward to reveal a vision of such beauty that Richard's breath caught, his engorged flesh growing ever more painful. Gone were her tight blue jeans and pink floral top. Instead, Rebeca had changed into a lacy, black robe that was tied around her narrow waist and barely covered her pale ivory thighs. She had also taken her hair out of its braid so that it cascaded down her back in a tangle of lustrous dark curls and framed her soft features.

She lit up at the sight of him. "Oh Mr Martin, thank God, I was starting to worry you weren't coming."

Once again, Alice's words echoed in his ears and Richard felt the heat rising in his cheeks as he realised he was staring. Flashing a hollow smile and praying she wouldn't notice the bulge straining against his right trouser leg, he said, "Rebecca, how many times have I asked you to call me Richard? Mr Martin makes me sound like some whining old geezer."

"Well, you are an old man, Mr Martin." Giggling playfully, she stepped aside to let him enter. "Would you like something to drink? Tea? Coffee?"

"Ahh…tea, milk and two sugars please and, *thanks*," he said, his voice dripping with sarcasm at the joke as he moved into the flat. The layout was almost identical to that of his and Alice's and he quickly moved down the hall into the Blaire's living room. With dim, off-cream walls and filled only by a small jumble of cheap mismatched furniture, it looked larger than it actually was.

A grubby old grey and blue denim sofa faced an even more ancient Panasonic television that had been mounted upon a near modern looking glass and steel stand that was certainly more functional than decorative. There was a single, three-tiered, mahogany veneer, bookcase, its shelves sagging under a dozen piles of dog-eared military and spy fiction paperbacks, a ceramic bowl atop a walnut look-alike end table under the window, as well as a massive opening night poster from the 80's hit-movie *Predator* that had been framed and hung on a wall. At the back of the room, a tall display case of solid teak stood in stark contrast to the items of veneered plywood scattered around it and held an impressive collection of Rebecca's swimming trophies. From a young age, the girl had been an avid swimmer and had even gone on to represent Gloucester in three county events, but after her parents' divorce, she had lost much of her enthusiasm for the sport. Now she rarely went more than once or twice a month.

The computer desk stood opposite the display case, the laptop already open and booting up. It was an ancient HP that hadn't been updated beyond Window's *Vista*. Sitting on the threadbare ottoman that the Blaire's employed as a chair and grimacing at the uncomfortable sensation in his semi-hard manhood, he logged into Rebecca's account and was immediately confronted by the problem as a virus conjured up an obviously falsified police lockdown. He tapped a few select keys, but to no effect. Next, he tried to open the start menu, but the virus brought up a warning box and cancelled the command. Finally, he logged out and entered Derik's account. The result was the same.

After a moment, Rebecca entered with his tea and placed it on an old *Top Gear* magazine lying beside the laptop. "Any luck?"

"Does this happen every time you log on?"

"Yes. It's been like this now for two days," she replied, her voice trembling as she peered far enough over his shoulder for him to taste her scent, reminding him of the first breath of spring. The scent steeled his length. "Can you fix it?"

Richard didn't answer. Instead, he pressed down on the power button until the screen went blank. Restarting the machine, he quickly switched to safe mode before letting it load up. Again, logging into the girl's profile, he waited a moment to make sure it didn't change again before going into its control panel and initiating a system restore to the pre-set point. It was a pretty routine trick that would work 99 times out of a 100. However, when he logged on for the third time, the scowling face of the law immediately opposed him.

"It might take a while."

Repeating the process of placing it in safe mode, he then filed through the recent system downloads and found that there were more than two hundred from the past thirty-six hours. He deleted them all, sipping his tea and cursing under his breath every time one or a dozen would randomly regenerate. When all of them were finally put down for good, he restarted the laptop and was finally met by Rebecca's normal background of a '*Hello Kitty*' poster.

Exhaling a long breath, he gratefully pushed away from the desk and stretched his legs out to relieve the cramp building in his knees. It felt like he'd been at the desk for hours, but his tea was still lukewarm, so it couldn't have been any more than twenty minutes.

Throwing one leg over and around the ottoman, he twisted to face the sofa where Rebecca was now reclining, watching some cheesy Jennifer Aniston rom-com that was playing on ITV2 whilst eating from a carton of ice cream. The sight of her soft pink lips wrapped around the spoon sent a hot pulse straight down his spine and he heard her moan in delight, her soft brown eyes falling closed as she savoured its sweetness…

"There you go Rebecca, all done."

"Really!" Startled out of her trance, her head whirled to face him and as she shifted, the lace of her gown moved with her, flashing him a momentary glimpse of her soft ivory bosom. "Ohhh…thank you, thank you, Mr Martin!"

"You're welcome, Rebecca." It was time to go; he knew it as well as he knew the desire stirring in his loins. And yet he could not will his legs to move. "But you should really consider updating your security, or perhaps switching to a more secure browser."

"I know we do. I keep telling Dad, but he just ignores me. He thinks it will cost too much money. Ohhh…thank you so much Mr Martin, I don't know what I would have done without you." Then, almost giddy and still clutching her carton of ice cream, she sprang up from her seat and raced across the room to throw her arms around him in a tight hug. The embrace caught Richard off guard, and he could do little more than bask in the feeling of her young body pressed against him. He could feel her breath on his neck, hot as a furnace and tickling his every weak spot as the sweetness of her scent filled his every breath, causing a fog to descend upon his mind.

Time seemed to slip away. He couldn't say for how long she clung to him, yet when she finally broke the embrace, he felt light-headed and she couldn't meet his gaze. A blush touched her cheeks pink, and she quickly stepped back. He should go now. This was his chance, before things got even more complicated; all he had to do was politely say goodbye, leave, and then everything would be fine…

Yet the moment came and went, and the silence hung between them as a heavy iron collar, binding them to each other.

"You're eating ice cream, what flavour?" he finally asked, desperate for anything that might ease the tension.

Rebecca, however, seemed to have forgotten all about the carton and it was only when she looked down and saw it there that she realised icy drops of condensation were running off her fingers. "Ohhh…it is Tesco's Cherrylicious." She had such a sweet voice. Why hadn't he ever noticed it before? "Would you like some?"

Damn, he had always had a weakness for cherries. He knew he shouldn't, yet when she offered him the spoon, its head filled with a blend of fluffy white vanilla and thick gooey cherry, he couldn't resist and obediently opened his mouth to accept the sweet treat. The taste of it flooded his senses, as deliciously bitter as it was sweet, and he swallowed it all greedily. Yet as she pulled the spoon away, a single creamy drop escaped the corner of his mouth and ran wetly down his chin. He moved to brush it aside, but Rebecca's spoon was quicker, and she scooped up the droplet before bringing it to her own lips.

"Mmm…delicious," she moaned, and he realised it wasn't the ice cream's bitter-sweet flavour she had tasted, but his own. Seeming to sense his scrutiny, she suddenly stilled, and when their eyes met, they both knew the truth.

Heart pounding, he reached out and took the utensil from her before hurling it aside with a flick of his wrist. Then they came together, and he could feel his head spinning as their lips met. Rebecca didn't hesitate; the ice cream carton was gone, discarded. He knew not where or when, and she was upon him, straddling his waist. Wrapping her arms around his neck, she kissed him hungrily, her lips parting and her small tongue pressing against his lips, demanding entry.

Richard knew he should stop this before things went too far, but his body was acting on its own and his mouth opened to accept her, passionately returning the kiss as his hands seized her backside and crushed her to him. *She tastes like…cherries.*

Surrendering to the moment, a low growl rumbled through him as he lost himself in the intoxicating sweetness of her lips. He could feel her breasts pressing against him as her tongue ran wild within his mouth, brushing over his teeth and tickling the roof of his orifice. She let out a small moan as his tongue slipped over hers and hotly twirled around the probing muscle, pressing it back into the warmth of her mouth. All too aware of his fully engorged arousal straining for release from its tight confines, he used his hold on her buttocks to draw her closer, letting her feel the effect she was having on him as their tongues danced. Whimpering with pleasure, Rebecca eagerly responded by rocking her hips against his own and a hot shiver ran down his spine as he felt the damp heat of her desire through the mesh of garments.

Only when his breath was exhausted, and the need for air utterly dire, did he break the kiss. Yet drunk on her sweetness, he couldn't stop; grabbing deep ragged breaths, he swooped down and began to nip a trail of fire from the sensitive spot just under her ear, down the soft slope of her neck, and to the exposed crook of her shoulder. Gasping hotly in a mixture of pleasure and pain at every tiny subtle bite, Rebecca tilted her head back, exposing more skin for him to kiss as her fingers tangled in his hair, a ragged moan escaping her as his tongue traced the ridge of her collarbone.

Richard didn't care that he was leaving marks, that the girl's neck was red and glistening; he couldn't stop, couldn't get enough. He was addicted to her taste, her scent, the softness of her skin, and even the very feel of her writhing against him drove him wild; but it wasn't enough.

Tight and firm, her lace covered buttocks filled his hands nicely and he couldn't resist squeezing the luscious mounds, making the beauty moan, before trailing his hands up along her sides, mentally mapping the sensual curves before hooking a finger over the robe's belt. With a quick tug, the tie came undone, and the garment fell open. Keeping one hand locked to her narrow waist, the other slid beneath the folds of the robe to explore the previously hidden delights. Softer than silk but hot to the touch, her skin trembled at his lightest contact and he ran his fingers teasingly over the bumps of her ribs before coming to her bosom.

His hand moulded to her left breast, eager digits kneading the soft, supple flesh whilst his thumb and forefinger rolled the pebbled nipple. Thrilled by his touch, she arched her back, pressing her cleavage further into his palm, and moaned in utter wonder as he trailed his tongue along her collarbone in small gentle kisses, soothing the bite marks, her fingers tugging at his hair each time his thumb playfully squeezed her pert bud.

"Oh Mr Martin…mmm…yessss…*harder*!" she gasped, her breathing ragged with barely suppressed moans, before bowing her head and plunging her tongue into his ear, arousing him further.

His cock jumping at the strange sensation, Richard growled before releasing his hold on her breast and rearing backwards, ceasing his attentions to her neck, drawing an all too audible whimper of protest from Rebecca. Paying no mind to her discontent, he reached up with both hands and pushed the robe off her shoulders and down her arms, leaving her flawless ivory skin naked to his eyes, except for a matching thong of black lace. He wantonly devoured the sight of her near naked beauty. Lithe and willowy, she had a swimmer's body and though he was accustomed to the sight of her flat stomach and long shapely legs, it was as if he were seeing her for the first time. Full and firm, her tear-drop shaped breasts rose and fell with her every breath. Their milky complexion contrasted perfectly with her dusky pink nipples.

"I know they're…not very big," admitted Rebecca, her voice flat and barely above a whisper, drawing his attention up to her face as she disentangled her fingers from his hair to cross her arms over her chest. She couldn't meet his gaze and all the confidence was leeching from her features to leave an unmistakable mask of doubt, perhaps even fear; fear that he might find her unsatisfactory or repulsive.

The very idea filled him with such sour emotion that he was almost overwhelmed by the urge to crush her to him and promise her she was beautiful. Instead, he raised his hand to her wrists and gently lowered her arms. "No Rebecca, they're perfect; you're perfect."

She looked at him in alarm, her eyes misty with tears, yet before she could speak, his lips touched hers in a kiss. It was sweet and tender, and she didn't resist. When he pulled away, she tried to follow, but he swooped down and took her right nipple between his lips, making her gasp in pleasure. She arched into his touch, giving him easier access to her ample cleavage as his tongue playfully circled her nipple, drawing tantalising rings of fire around the stiff bud before sensually grazing it with his teeth.

"Ohhh…Mr Martin!" she moaned; he could feel her rocking earnestly against the bulge of his arousal. Her small hands moved to claw at his head, seizing great clumps of his raven locks before running down his neck and roaming the broad plane of his shoulders and back, his muscles bunching and contracting at the feel of her nails scraping through the thin cotton of his shirt. Shivering in a mix of pleasure and agony at her sharp touch, his hand moved back up to roughly knead her neglected breast while his lips continued their assault. No longer teasing, he began to suckle ravenously, his tongue skilfully flicking across her nipple while the rough pad of his thumb massaged its twin, enjoying the way she responded to his every touch.

No match for such an onslaught, Rebecca's head tipped back. She uttered a torrent of delightful sounds as she basked in the sensations he was stirring within her. Moaning and writhing against the trapped bulge of his arousal, her hands fumbled with the buttons of his shirt, her digits clumsy from her inexperience and desperation to rid him of the garment. When the last popped free, the shirt fell open and her hand moved down between their bodies, cupping the weight of his cock through his trousers.

"So-so big…" she gasped out hotly and he couldn't help uttering a low moan against her breast at the feeling of her fingers closing around him, her palm jerking up and down as she massaged his length. "Ooh God; please…take me to bed, Mr Martin!"

With his mind fogged by lust, Richard couldn't resist her and released her breast before seizing her buttocks with both hands and standing up from the ottoman. Squealing with delight, Rebecca crossed her legs over his waist and wrapped her arms securely around his neck, effectively clinging to him for dear life as he hoisted her up and carried her out of the living room and into the darkened hallway. Though this was the first time he'd been in this part of the Blaire's flat, as its layout was identical to that of his own, it was easy for him to navigate the gloom of the narrow antechamber towards the minor bedroom at its end, which he guessed was Rebecca's. He was tempted to try for the handle, but the feeling of Rebecca's lips on his neck persuaded him there was no time. One good kick was all he needed to have the door swing open.

Chapter Four

Rebecca's room was bright and vibrant, with pale blue wallpaper and polished pine furnishings. Framed posters of various animals hung on the walls, as well as a wall-mounted *Sony* combi, LCD television and DVD player, and a divan double bed that dominated one corner of the room. Approaching the side of the bed, he dropped her unceremoniously upon the divan, causing the girl to squeal with alarm, before stepping back and shrugging off his shirt. As the garment pooled around his feet, he felt goosebumps erupting over his arms as the chilly air touched his skin. Despite the cold, the ache in his groin had grown almost unbearable, and he quickly stepped out of his shoes and socks before pushing both his trousers and boxers down his legs, sighing with relief as his painfully stiff erection burst free of its confines.

Rebecca could only gasp, her big doe eyes shamelessly drinking in the sight of his masculinity before a hungry smile turned her lips. Feeling the heat of her gaze lingering upon him, Richard couldn't resist smirking before moving to join her on the black sheets. Relishing the image of her spread out beneath him, his eyes fixed on his last obstacle. Reaching out, he hooked his fingers under the hem of her panties, now visibly damp and glistening with dew, and dragged the sodden garment down her legs, leaving her completely exposed to his ravenous gaze.

Visibly trembling, Rebecca opened her legs, inviting him to continue. His mouth watering at the sight of her sex, he tossed the garment aside before leaning forward, drawn by the heady scent of her arousal, to hover above her folds.

"Mr Martin?" Her breath was shaky with need and impatience, as she watched him. "What are you do-ohhh!" The words fell into a long moan as his mouth descended upon her.

Plunged into a world of sensory delights, he thrust his tongue into her molten depths, stroking her plush inner-walls. She had a spiced, tangy flavour, and he was immediately addicted.

"Mmm…that feels so good…Mr Martin…" gasped Rebecca, her sweet voice breathless with pleasure as his tongue explored her channel. Savouring the taste of her,

Richard held nothing back and ate her greedily. His tongue lapped and twirled, drawing a maze of intricate patterns across her inner walls before suddenly withdrawing between his jaws, only to plunge deeper into her centre.

Her hips jumped against him and he glanced up to see her head rolling back, her eyes closed and mouth open in a long moan. Grinning inwardly at the look of pleasure etched upon her features, he slid her legs over his shoulders before seizing her buttocks, supporting her weight easily, and drawing her closer while swirling his tongue around the deepest part of her, making her buck and cry with pleasure.

"Ohhhhhhhh!!!" she moaned before seizing white knuckled handfuls of the sheets, her hips rolling wantonly against his mouth, demanding more.

"Mmm…you're delicious," he murmured against her flesh, rolling his tongue to the rhythm of her body and feeling his cock jump as her sounds of pleasure sent a pulse of electrified excitement coursing through his nerves. Absorbing everything he was doing to her, Rebecca could only writhe and moan as her senses were overloaded and he could feel the mounting tension within her as she approached her heavenly summit.

Far from finished with her, however, Richard withdrew his tongue from her heat and drew it gently up her folds to teasingly circle her clitoris before closing his mouth over the beauty's swollen bud, a grin crossing his thin lips at her sudden cry of rapture.

"Ohhh-shit-yesss!" she shrieked, her big brown eyes dark with lust, widening to the size of saucers as his lips wrapped around the tiny bud and drew it into the heat of his mouth, suckling it. When his tongue flicked it, slender fingers tangled in his hair, dragging him closer as her hips bucked wildly against his orifice. "Ugh-right there...don't stop-ahhh-yes, yes, yes, YES!"

He focused all his attention on that small bundle of nerves, delighting in her cries of ecstasy while skilfully swirling his tongue over and around, switching randomly between sharp licks and teasing rolls again and again; keeping her purposefully on edge as the sweet oblivion welled up within her. Clearly unprepared for the rush of sensations, Rebecca could do little more than gasp and pant and cry out in delight, her fingers tugging urgently at his hair whilst her hips bucked and rolled beneath his sinfully wicked motions.

And then, suddenly, the truth of his situation caught up to him.

Ohhh God...*what the hell am I doing!* Richard thought, yet all the while unable to resist admiring the way her body danced as his tongue expertly jabbed at her clit, his firm grip holding her in check even as she strained for more. This wasn't him. Richard Martin never cheated; he was a loyal husband who loved his wife. He didn't do things like this, he couldn't, it wasn't right...

Desperately, he tried to conjure up a vision of Alice but the image of her seemed to linger just out of memory, dancing before his gaze within a haze of smoke and mist before a sharp, agonising pain shot along the length of his erection, reminding him of his own pressing need. Beaten, his body acted on its own accord and he caught the bundle of nerves between his teeth while humming a low rumbling *"Mmm..."*

"Ohhh right there…right there-oh God-ughhh I'm cumming...oh God-oh God-ohhh goooohhhhhhhh!!!" Rebecca cried, losing all control, deliriously thrashing her head and arching off the sheets; her whole body trembling with the force of the climax ripping through her. Unchecked, Richard worked her down from the heights before gently lowering her onto the bed, her eyes falling shut as she basked in the wondrous aftermath. This was his chance. It wasn't too late. All he had to do was get dressed and leave, now.

Yet his brain was fogged, and his limbs wouldn't move. He was standing on the bank of the *Rubicon*. Should he cross its depths, there would be no turning back, he would be lost, adrift in purgatory, and everything he loved would be at stake, forfeit. If Alice were to learn of it, their marriage would be over, his son would grow up to despise him, friends and family would shun him like a stray dog. And yet, could he live with himself if he didn't, knowing he'd come this far only to turn away, and always wondering what it would have been like?

But then the decision was taken out of his hands. Flushed and panting, Rebecca's eyes fluttered open, and she looked up at him dreamily. "Come on, come on…don't stop now. Ohhh God, I'm so hot. Please fuck me, Mr Martin! I need you to fuck me…"

How could he resist?

Alea iacta est.

Crawling up the length of her body, covering her slender frame as he rose above her and settled between her splayed legs. He didn't worry about a condom; he knew Rebecca had been on the pill since her sixteenth birthday. Alice had taken her to the hospital to get a prescription. Seeing the lust burning in those innocent doe eyes, the last of his resistance melted away, and he plunged into her molten core.

"Ohhh," Rebecca moaned at the sudden invasion, her eyes widening and head rolling back into the mess of tangled sheets as he entered her, burrowing inside bit-by-bit, filling her completely.

"Ughhh…" Richard groaned once he was completely embedded within her liquid heat, almost losing himself in the feeling of inner walls stretching and wrapping around his engorged flesh. The urge to move was so overwhelming that it took every bit of his willpower to remain still, relishing the feel of her tight embrace as he drew in deep ragged breaths and waited for her to adjust to his size. He'd known she wasn't a virgin for some time; but she was still so tight and though he was far from huge, he must have been considerably larger than what she was accustomed to. The realisation sent a delightful thrill down his spine, and his cock twitched.

"Ahhh…" cried the girl, her inner muscles tensing around him so tightly that he was afraid he'd hurt her and began to withdraw. "No! Don't stop. Do it again…."

His cock throbbed dangerously at her words and the slick snugness of her walls made him pant as he began to rock his hips. He moved in small rowing motions, delighting in the friction between their bodies. Arching beneath him as he rolled his hips, Rebecca seized his buttocks with both hands, her fingernails digging into his flesh before dragging trails of fire up his lower back as her legs wrapped around his flanks, crossing at the ankles, and urging him to go deeper while rocking urgently against his gentle motions.

"Ooohhhh God! Give it to me Mr Martin…I want it…I want it…ahhhhh-yes-yesss" Her words fell into an endless stream of moans and gasps as he drew back until just the bulbous head remained encased within her, before thrusting back into her hard and fast. She jumped at his intrusion, her delicate insides rippling and convulsing around his hard length, trying to draw him deeper. Enjoying the feel of her squirming beneath him, he repeated the motion, again and again, building a steady rhythm that had him delving deeper with every thrust. He'd meant to be slow and gentle, to take it easy on her, but she had proved his undoing in that first delicious instant.

He felt maddened, bewitched, and so utterly out of control. Lust burned hot and molten through his veins, and just the sight of her writhing beneath him, wantonly begging for more, was nearly too much for him to bear. Suddenly there was nothing gentle in his motions, just a desperate, unyielding need.

"Ughhh…so-so tight," he growled; his voice choked with pleasure as he thrust back inside her plush passage, filling her completely, the feeling of her inner walls squeezing his returning flesh almost pitching him over the edge and he knew he wouldn't last much longer. It had been over a month since he and Alice last had sex, and the torment of the night's games had left his cock so sensitised he thought it might burst at any moment. *But not yet. Not yet!*

"Ohhh fuck…your dick feels so good…oh-oh-ohhh…don't stop…don't stop!" cried Rebecca, eagerly meeting every one of his downward strokes with an upward roll of her hips, her nails clawing madly at his back each time his pelvis grazed her clit. He was certain she was leaving marks, but at this point, it was hard to be concerned about anything, even of discovery by his loving wife, who was waiting for him in the flat below them.

"Mmm…So is this what you want, Rebecca?" Fighting to ignore the rush of pleasure creeping up his spine as he plunged into the deepest parts of the beauty, Richard held nothing back, hastening his thrusts until the bed beneath them seemed to be rocking to their wild rhythm. The sound of it all was music to his ears; the squeaking of bedsprings, the wet slapping of flesh on flesh and, of course, Rebecca's overwhelmed moans.

"Yes, yes...it was always you...I've always wanted you, Mr Martin...Oh God! Feels so good, fuck me harder...HARDER!" A cry of rapturous delight tore from her lips as his hips snapped in deep, long strokes that made her spine curl and her breasts bounce. Like him, she was nearing her peak. He could feel the balls of her feet beating against his arse, urging him to push her over that summit she so desperately yearned to reach.

Somewhere, buried deep in the depths of his subconscious, a part of him dreaded that inevitable conclusion, perhaps still hoping that this was all some wonderful, but monstrous nightmare and that his failure would banish this all away, like a foul odour on a great gust of wind. He might even have felt guilty for using the girl so thoughtlessly, had she not been writhing wantonly beneath him, meeting him thrust for thrust and begging for more. But he had come too far to stop now.

Feeling his release building, his sanity hanging by a thread; he reared back, his hands coming up to seize the swells of her buttocks, hoisting her off the sheets and pulling her firmly against him as he continued to thrust into her wildly. Inhaling sharply at this new angle, Rebecca's head rolled back in a voiceless cry and her hands fell away to brace against at the wall, searching desperately for some kind of purchase while doing her best to match his furious rhythm.

"Ah...ahhh-oh my God-oh my God-oh my God...I can't take it... it's too much...too big!" she shrieked, her fingers clawing at the walls and eyes wide with pure ecstasy. "Oh yes...yesssss...don't stop...I'm all yours Mr Martin...I've wanted your hard cock inside me for so long...you can fuck me whenever you want to...just don't stop...don't stop!"

The room was thick with the musky scent of sex. Grunting as he surged inside her, Richard savoured the sight of her pleasure-drunk features as his hands, roughly kneading her tight young arse like dough, guided her motions in time with his own. Spurred on by her heated encouragements, and the wondrous feeling of her molten channel writhing around his sensitised organ, he slammed into her mercilessly. His back was afire and he could feel beads of sweat rolling down his brow as he thrust hard and fast between her silky thighs, working tirelessly to push them both off their approaching peaks, the tingling sensation down in the base of his spine warning him of his impending oblivion.

"Ohhhh God...I can feel it...I'm going to cum.... fuck me, fuck meeeeee!" Rebecca cried, racing towards another climax and sobbing with pleasure while thrashing her head from side to side. "Ohhh-yes-yes...I'm cummingaahhhhhhhh!" her voice dissolved into a shrill cry of pleasure, and her inner walls erupted, convulsing around his thick length in a wash of molten warmth as she rode the orgasm, quivering and bucking against him uncontrollably.

Richard groaned in primitive delight, teetering on the brink, watching avidly as she came undone before the feelings the girl was stirring finally proved too much and a thunderous roar burst from his jaws. Slamming into her one last time, he felt something deep inside his abdomen contract and pulse, and then there was only the fire coursing through his veins as he released his essence into her warmth.

Exhausted beyond measure, they collapsed together in a heap on the bed.

Breathing hard and trembling with miniature aftershocks, Richard had just enough sense left to roll off the beauty, withdrawing his softening arousal from her still vivacious channel. Whimpering at the feeling of emptiness, Rebecca curled into his flank, the feeling of her nestling against him, drawing a low moan from the exhausted man as all notion of time slipped away. For several long moments, he was content to just bask in the glow of a much-needed release. Sleep's warm embrace dragging him down to that peaceful abyss...

He jerked at the sensation of falling, shattering the spell and leaving him cold, naked, and very much awake.

I need a shower. It was a strange thought. He knew he should have felt guilty, afraid, and perhaps even sick to his stomach, but oddly, a sense of calm detachment seemed to have settled over him and all he could really think about was how clammy his skin felt as the sheen of sweat covering him began to dry. He felt movement against his arm and glanced over to see Rebecca sleeping peacefully beside him, with an arm draped over his front and her head resting peacefully on his shoulder. She was smiling contentedly.

Chapter Five

"I have to go." He had tried to say it softly, so as to avoid disturbing her entirely, but his throat was dry and what came out was a raspy parody of a voice. Her body quivered in surprise at the sound and her eyes fluttered open, glassy with unshed tears.

"But...but can't you stay with me tonight?"

"You know I can't." In truth, he would have liked nothing better than to stay with her, but he knew Alice would be growing worried and it wouldn't be long before she came looking for him. The thought of her finding them like this sent the first true shiver of fear down his spine, and with the idea of her barging through the door, dressed like Rambo and armed with enough firepower to orbit Schwarzenegger in mind, he gently pushed her aside and sat up. Rising to his feet, he quickly set about collecting the garments that were scattered across the floor. Yet his mind was only half on the task, and as a result, he had done up more than half of his shirt's buttons before realising two of them were in the wrong hole. Even so, he couldn't keep from cringing when the cloth touched his back. The skin there felt painfully raw and inflamed; he'd need to be careful Alice didn't see the marks for a couple of days.

Finally dressed, though appearing curiously dishevelled, he straightened up and was about to leave when he heard the rustle of bedsheets.

"Please…Richard, promise me this wasn't just a one-night stand," Rebecca called out and despite his better judgement, he glanced back and his heart nearly broke at the vision of her sitting there, desperately trying to hide her nakedness by clutching the soiled sheets to her chest, her ivory skin almost glowing and big doe eyes sparkling pleadingly. Even after such a thorough fucking, she was no less a vision of innocence and purity, the sweetest of temptations.

"We'll see," he said, trying to keep his voice flat and features stern, hiding the sudden stab of emotion in his chest. He left without a backwards glance, shutting the bedroom door firmly behind him, doing his best to ignore Rebecca's tearful sobs.

Sweet
Temptations:
THE BOSS'S DAUGHTER

THE LORD OF LUST
L.M. MOUNTFORD

Sweet Temptations:

THE BOSS'S DAUGHTER

L.M. MOUNTFORD

Prologue

His back burned and the spray cut clean to the bone as fat wet snakes slithered down his arms and legs, so cold they burned.

Eyes hooded and vacant, Richard watched the run-off collect around the shower drain, swirling around and around. The blood was almost washed away, leaving only long accusing fingers of dark crimson streaking across the porcelain.

Time had lost all meaning. Seconds and hours bled together until…

"Goddamnit!"

He wanted to scream. To shout. To bellow like a bear in a cage, being dragged through the streets for the amusement of a medieval mob, roaring and bawling in a show of futile outrage at the hard, inescapable reality. Yet the pitiful grunt was all he dared with Alexander in the next room, liable to stir at the smallest sound, and Alice sleeping peacefully just across the hall. So instead, he took it out on the shower wall the way an angry child would beat a pillow.

Red-hot knives stabbed between his knuckles and up his arm in a blast of near-crippling agony as he hit the wall hard enough for bone to crack against the porcelain. Regardless, he ground his knuckles into the tile, relishing the agony it induced, needing it and not knowing what else to do.

Then the moment was gone, and Richard was left shivering in the cold, hot tears stinging his eyes. "Wh-what the fuck have I done?" The question rang hollow, even to his ears.

What had he done? He'd fucked his babysitter, a girl almost young enough to be his daughter. He'd cheated on his wife. And, what was worse, he'd loved every fucking second of it. Then he'd fled.

He could still hear Rebecca crying in her room.

Her sobs had chased him out of the Blaire's flat like a pack of hounds snapping at his heels and it had been all he could do to make it back to the flat without breaking his neck. Alice had already gone to bed when he came bursting through the door. Deep down, a more rational part of him was relieved he didn't have to explain to his instinctively suspicious wife why he was getting in so late, or the fact he smelt like sex and his shirt was misbuttoned, but in that moment, all he could think about was a shower. He'd barely spared a moment to look into their bedroom to check on her before jumping into the bath and cranking the water temperature as low as it would go.

Goddammit! What the fuck had he done! Why had he even gone to fix the computer in the first place? It wasn't a vital job. Rebecca might have been in a state, but it could have waited until morning. So, why the fuck had he gone to the fix the bloody computer, when he'd known, he'd just known it was a bad idea.

Alarm bells had gone off the moment Alice had suggested the girl fancied him. He would have pressed her for more, but then she kissed him, and his world had dissolved to just the feeling of her luscious body pressing into his.

It had been much the same the night they first met, when she'd cornered him in The Burning Book's storeroom. He'd been getting a fresh crate of beer when he'd noticed her leaning against the door. He hadn't noticed her slipping in after him, and the sight of the tiny brunet, all curves and smiles in a black wrap-around dress that could only have been painted on, standing there with her hand on her hip almost had him jumping out of his skin.

Only the Lord alone knew how he managed not to drop the bottles in each hand.

Her smile had only grown more sinful when he'd told her she was in a staff-only area. Then, with a cock of her head and a pouting moan, she'd been on him and he'd promptly forgotten all of his fears of getting caught.

Richard would have stayed. He would have, but then Alice's remarks about Rebecca rung in his ears. Suddenly, he couldn't get the girl out of his head and he'd felt so ashamed that he just needed to get away.

The irony of it all did not escape him.

Self-loathing twisting his guts, he opened and closed his fist, working the feeling back into the stiff digits. They all moved. That was good, nothing broken, but they hurt pretty bad and the throbbing in the knuckles was enough to make him wince with each flex. Then again, that was good too. He deserved the pain.

Christ, I need a drink.

The thought came from out of nowhere but had a restorative effect that had Richard thumbing the shower panel. Pulling the curtain back before the deluge had ceased, he stepped out of the bath, grabbed a towel off the rail and, heedless of the water still running down his legs, made straight for the kitchen.

The oven's display showed it was just after two in the morning.

Out of habit, he made to fill the kettle, but then at the last minute opened the top cabinet. The British Empire might have been built on tea, but this called for something stronger. And he needed to get royally shit faced. Rummaging through the various jars, bottles, and tins, he retrieved the mostly full Bushmills they kept for when Alice's parents came to visit, before grabbing a glass from the draining board.

Pouring himself a measure, Richard threw his head back and downed the whiskey. It burned all the way down, but the liquor brought the warmth back, lessening the sickening knot rooted in his gut, so he savoured it all the same, relishing the hard flavour and distinctive aroma that curled up his nose-

"C-C-Christ," he bit out, coughing so violently each breath rasped like sandpaper, and his hand shook as he filled the glass again. This time making it a double, he stowed the bottle, and its now notably emptied contents, back into the cupboard before exiting the kitchen, drink in hand.

The living room had lost all its warmth as Richard half-sat, half-collapsed onto the sofa. Bathed in the soft light of the standing lamp they kept on a timer to dissuade thieves from getting ambitious, inky blackness pooled along the edges of the walls. Long shadows stretched across the floor like the bars of a cell. His cell.

Wary of another coughing fit that might rouse his wife, he only nursed the drink, sipping the dark amber liquid while staring over the rim of the glass at the dark outside the window.

What have I done?

Hardly a frequent or heavy drinker, the Bushmills made his eyes heavy and his head feel light as the alcohol took effect. The question haunted him, ringing through his ears while flashbacks of the last hour played out before his eyes.

His cock stiffened at the memory of Rebecca standing in the doorway in nothing but that robe. The way her slender curves rigged in his lap. The taste of her on his lips. Her breathy pleading as he tongued her clit. The feeling of her tight little cunt exploding around him...

He hated himself for what he'd done. He'd cheated on Alice, broken his vows to her and risked their marriage. He'd used Rebecca, fucked her like a bitch in heat. Then, worse still, discarded her so callously even though he knew, well suspected, she had feelings for him.

God in fucking hell, he was a beast.

A part of him still couldn't believe it. Here in the safety of his home, on his sofa with a glass of whiskey, the night felt like a bad dream. A God damn fucking nightmare. Only he'd woken to it. The night was like a dream he could only half remember, slipping out of his grasp like pale wisps of morning mist curling around his fingers whenever he tried to focus on one moment. All except for those moments. They were sharp and clear and played before his eyes whenever he'd closed them.

What the fuck was wrong with him? He and Alice were finally getting their lives back to a sense of normality… How was he going to look her in the eye again, knowing that he'd… Christ, what would she say? What would she do? He'd ruined everything. And just when it had all seemed to be going so well. In layman's terms-

"I'm fucked." He toasted the declaration by downing the rest of his Bushmills. "Oh God. *Al*, I'm sor-"

The timer on the lamp's plug clicked over, cutting the power.

Darkness consumed him.

Chapter One

There was comfort in sleep. The fool and coward's comfort. The comfort of hiding in the dark and fooling himself it had all been a dream.

Caught between sleeping and waking, Richard stared up at the ceiling. Autumn morning half-light crept through the curtains over the bed, turning their bedroom dark and grey. He didn't hear the cars speeding down Stroud Road, trying to beat the early morning rush hour, or the occasional gurgles coming through the baby monitor. Nor see the furniture taking shape in the gloom. He didn't want to wake up.

He wanted to sleep and dream and pretend. Better that than face reality and the consequences of what he'd done. Having to see his wife every day, holding her in his arms, making love to her, looking into her eyes, seeing the love there, and knowing, just knowing, he'd betrayed her.

Yes, he didn't want to wake, but the warm body wriggling beside him made it inevitable…

He blinked when a hand brushed up his side. Long, delicate fingers, feeling up his ribs and across his stomach. Then there was only softness and warmth. And a faint hint of cinnamon.

A sideways glance showed Alice sleeping next to him on a bed of her mahogany tresses. She must have rolled onto his side sometime in the night and, half covered by the quilt, was curling into him, head resting on his shoulder. She looked so peaceful. Content. Utterly oblivious to everything that had taken place through the night.

Her peace tore at him. Yet he was captivated and watched her sleep regardless, her delicate beauty enrapturing him the way the radiance of the moon enslaves a wolf.

He had to tell her, but how? A part of him wanted to confess now and have done with it. To wait would only make things harder, more complicated.

Excuses flitted through his mind. He was drunk. He'd been desperate. It hadn't meant anything. It was the usual line-up of dirt-bag husband excuses. Though he made sure to steer WELL clear of anything even hinting Alice bore some responsibility. That would not go down well.

Once, he even contemplated suggesting Rebecca had instigated it all. That got chucked out as quickly as it came. No matter what, he needed to keep the girl out of this.

As fond as she was of their babysitter, Richard knew his wife well enough to know she did not share her toys. And if that confrontation with Scarlet last night had just been Alice marking her territory...

Then, he had a pretty good idea of what she would do to him.

That thought made the idea of letting her sleep in a little longer, all the more tempting.

"Alice..." he mumbled. She'd think it odd if he didn't wake her. It would make her suspicious…

Alice mumbled something unintelligible in answer. Still more or less asleep, she shifted closer to nuzzle the hollow of his neck.

Richard stiffened at the contact, a shiver of pleasure rippling up his spine.

Her very closeness was an aphrodisiac. The feeling of her pressed against him, long willowy legs brushing over his calf, full breasts crushed against his side through her cropped sleeping sweater. And her mouth. God, that wicked mouth, brushing so softly over his skin, a mere tease of contact, igniting and sending tingling sensations surging through his skin down to the base of his spine.

Suddenly awake, alert, and very aware of that tale-tell stirring between his legs, Richard blinked, then glanced down to see blue-green eyes looking up at him.

For the longest moment, Alice only watched him, lips pursed and eyes bright with a look that had his cock suddenly harder than steel. Then, slowly, she pivoted, propping her head up enough to rest her chin on his ribs. "When did you get in?"

"Late." The vision of her had the words sticking to the back of his throat. "Did you wait long?"

She moaned a low throaty affirmative, placing a soft kiss just above his nipple while, in a tease of friction, one deliciously long leg slid across to straddle his thigh, making Richard all the more aware of the feeling of her body on his. And the dampness pushing against his leg. She was soaked. The silky heat of her arousal burned through her panties as she stretched out, caging him beneath her, as she walked soft butterfly kisses up his torso.

"I couldn't sleep," Alice purred, her words low and throaty without a trace of sleep. She bit down on his earlobe and tugged, fingers teasing down the flat of his stomach to his boxers. "I just kept thinking about you pushing me up against the fridge, grinding this big, hard cock into my pussy." Long fingers closed around him through the cotton of his underwear, holding, squeezing, then rubbing. "It got me so hot. In the end, I needed Antonio…"

Richard had to bite back a moan. Antonio was Alice's name for the B.O.B her friend Samantha had bought them as a gag gift for their 5-year anniversary. The image of his wife stretched out on their bed, her luscious body arching in throes of pleasure as she worked the toy between her legs, turned his cock to steel within her grasp. Until he recalled just what he had been doing while she had been putting on such an exquisite display and the knot of guilt that lodged inside his gut threatened to chase his erection away.

Alice's mouth claimed his, her tongue sweeping in with lush licks that sent tingles shivering up his spine and brought him back to full mast.

She took his mouth hungrily, her lips moving over his, full and soft and completely at odds with the hot demand that seemed at once to make his head spin while keeping his attention fixed solely on her. And all the while, she was stroking him. Slowly, her tiny hand unable to encompass his girth, but pumping him from root to tip in long, knowing motions, had him instinctively rocking into her, grinding his groin against her palm.

God, how did she always know? Know just how to touch him, how to play his body like a fiddle?

It was maddening. He needed to touch her, but no sooner had his fingers swept through the lush fall of silky locks to tease over her spine than she pulled back.

"I-it got me so horny," she panted, trailing hot little kisses down the line of his jaw. "Knowing you could barge in at any moment and catch me playing with Antonio. I wanted you to watch, to see what you did to me, see how wet I got thinking about your big dick," she spoke slowly, every low throaty syllable an intoxicating seduction. "I was right here, riding my B.O.B, waiting for you to come and see what a naughty wife you have. But you never came. Then I remembered you were up there with Rebecca. Is that why you left me all alone?" Her mouth was everywhere, kissing every bit of skin she could reach as she shuffled slowly back...

Her tongue dragged over his nipple, down the plane of his chest to the elastic of his shorts, only to pull away. "A-Alice..."

His wife rose slowly to sit straight backed between his legs, throwing the covers off, and pushing the lush fall of her hair back behind her ears, the pink of her tongue sliding across those full lips as her eyes found his. Then, "Was she a bad girl for you?"

Oh fuck!

"What?" Ice rushed down his spine and it was all Richard could do to keep the panic from his voice. Fuck, she knew. How could he have been so stupid? Of course, Alice knew. How could she not? Now he was-

"Was she a bad girl?" Alice said again, her voice seeming to grow even more playful as she leaned down to where his erection was visibly straining against the confines of his shorts, the slick tip pushing up from beneath the elastic to leave a slick and shiny trail around his belly button. "Was she still wearing that sexy outfit she had on last night? That cute little pink top and those faded jeans."

Warm air rushed over his crown as those full luscious lips wrapped around him through his underwear and slid up to bite the waistband and tug it back to reveal the fullness of his desire. "Or had she changed into something different, something special, for your eyes only? Stockings? High heels. Maybe a pink babydoll-mmm…" She licked him. The point of her tongue slid slowly up the centre of his column in a long drag from base to tip. "Did you like seeing her like that? Flaunting her body for you in a naughty nighty, her ass and legs on full display, those lush tits peeking out, begging to be sucked. And what about her pussy, that tight, juicy little pussy? Did she taste good?"

Mouth dry and desire shivering through him, Richard couldn't stop the words, "So-so goo-oohh!"

Lips stretched wide and checks hollowed, Alice took the head into her mouth and sucked him greedily. She took her time, going neither fast nor slow, but with all the determination of a woman who loved giving head and wasn't afraid to let the world know it.

In a dark corner of his brain, Richard knew he should be disgusted with himself. Alice thought they were playing. To her, this was just a game to spice up the mood. She had no way of knowing he had been balls deep inside their neighbour's daughter last night. And to top it all off, instead of confessing his sin, he was letting her give him one hell of a blow job. But he couldn't resist. It had been so long since he'd felt those luscious lips wrapped around his dick. And her eyes...

Fuck, Alice's eyes were incredible. Deep and stormy, they seemed to shift between grey and blue depending on her mood, and he could stare into them for an eternity and never look away. There were times she had brought him to the brink of cumming with just a look.

It was at once too intense, yet not enough, and Richard had to fist the sheets against the urge to grab, claw, and drive her mouth all the way down on his cock. The lush heat of her mouth glided along his shaft, never taking more than an inch or two in. And so slow. Damnit, how can she be so slow...

"A-Alice..."

She pulled off just as slowly, her eyes burning into his all the way. "Mmm-did you make her your new little cock whore? I bet she was just begging for this big dick." She fluttered her tongue over the slit, making his whole cock tingle and his butt clench. Then she was licking him, that little pink tongue sliding up and down his length. "Did you make her beg for your cock?"

He couldn't think or focus on anything but the feel of her tongue. Then she was taking him back into the delicious heat of her mouth, her head bobbing up and down, the delicious suction of those full lips sliding along his shaft, drawing him deeper. It was too much.

"Yes."

Alice moaned her approval, her eyes bright and burning into his as she pulled off. With one small hand still stroking him, she crawled on all fours up the length of his body, slowly, with her body low and back just that bit arched so he could feel the weight of her breasts dragging up his belly, soft and warm through her thin cotton cardigan, before she reared, like Aphrodite rising from her pool to straddle his waist.

"Oh, you're so bad," she purred, and gave him one final stroke before bringing her fingers up to her mouth and sucked them clean with a low moan. "Mmm… I can taste her on your cock. Did she drop to her knees and suck your big, yummy, married dick first? Or did you just bend her over and fuck her brains out?"

Jesus, her games were going to kill him. "N-neither, I-oh…"

The words trailed away in a low moan as she rolled her hips, sliding his cock along her folds through her soaked panties, showing him how wet she'd gotten. Then, with her right hand, she hooked two fingers beneath the garment and pulled it back, exposing her pussy to his gaze.

"Mmm… yeah baby, what did you do?" Alice purred, taking his cock in her left hand and coating his crown in her cream before pressing it hard against her clit with a slow roll-

She stilled, that sweet little mouth dropping in a voiceless gasp as Richard's hands seized her hips and held her fast as he began working his thick crest into her moist heat. "This."

He'd had enough.

Breath seething, Richard could barely contain himself as he pulled her to him. Even after all their years together, and the birth of their son, she was still so deliciously snug, and he could feel her plush walls stretch as he filled her inch by inch until she'd sheathed to the hilt. The perfect fit for his cock.

"Oh… Oh god! Baby wa-wait…" Alice gasped, her eyes unfocused. Reaching back, she grasped his knees to brace herself. "Not so… you're too… too-oh god!"

Breathless, Richard could only nod, her slight movement altering his angle of penetration. It wasn't much. Just enough to send a rush of sensation up his spine as her slick, velvety walls wrapped around his cock, pulsing and sucking him in as deep as he could go.

The prior night was gone and done. Now it was only them and he bit, chewed, and clawed against the instinctive urge to throw his wife on the bed and just take her. It had been weeks since the last time they'd gone a few rounds. She'd need time, time to adjust, time to get used to the feeling of being filled with him. So instead Richard just watched her, drinking in the sight of Alice straddling him, her head tipped back, the bounty of lush mahogany tresses cascading down to the small of her back, the plunging neckline of her cardigan revealing a feast of golden skin as her breasts strained against the cotton, imprisoned from his view by a few struggling buttons.

He wanted to see more. He wanted to see her.

"Mmm… you feel amazing, so tight," he purred, reaching up to tug the button from its fastening, bearing her full and luscious cleavage. "And such beautiful tits."

"Yeah, better than hers?" Alice panted, her back curling in offering as he sat up and took the peak of a single dusky nipple into his mouth.

"Much."

He teased her mercilessly, raining soft kisses down across her breasts, his wily tongue lashing down and around, refusing to pay her nipple any attention. Her skin was growing hot and he could feel her shake in his arms, pleading for more. Yet she held on until he sucked the stiff peak into his mouth, his hands crushing her to him and grinding her down on his cock with just the right amount of force to make her creamy walls pulse around him.

"Liar."

Low and breathy, the heat in her words sent a shiver straight down his spine, moments before long fingers fisted in hair and dragged his head back. Dark and lustful, Alice's eyes burned hungrily into his as she lowered her full lips to his, her lush tongue claiming him in a possessive dance that both thrilled and terrified him. This wasn't part of her game. She wanted him to know he was hers. Her husband. Her lover. He was her man, no matter what, and he'd better not forget it.

She rolled her hips, breaking the kiss and rising until only half of him remained inside her.

"Mmm… Mr Martin," a soft, girlish voice purred. His heart leaping into his throat, Richard's eyes shot up to meet Rebecca's big doe eyes, his wife's sharp, angular face now soft and long. Then, she dropped back down, her lush heat clenching down, like a second mouth sucking him in...

Bolting upright, Richard just managed to brace himself on the armrests of his chair as it righted itself and almost pitched him headfirst into his desk. What the-

Reality caught up with him. He wasn't at home. He was at work in his office.

Sweating, heart pounding and his cock straining against his trousers, he collapsed back into the treacherous piece of furniture. Cupping his hands over his head and dragging his fingers down his face, he did his best to bite down on a sarcastic laugh. "Thank God. Just a dream-"

"Yo Dick, you feeling alright mate?"

Chapter Two

It never ceased to amaze Richard how, even when dressed to meet Holmes & Raine's business dress code, Mark McClaine always had the look of a second-hand car salesman. It was his perpetual grin. With that boot polish-black hair and moustache, it made him look like John Challis's Boycie in Only Fools and Horses, just without the sincerity.

Perched in the open door with his arms crossed, he was grinning at Richard like the cat that had got the cream. "Not looking too good there, Dick. Everything okay at home?"

"Yeah, I'm fine mate." Richard forced a smile. "Just, just got a lot on my mind, that's all."

Mark gave a dry laugh. Then, still grinning, he straightened and strolled over to his desk, the closest to the door, and dropped into his chair. He spun it around to face Richard in the adjoining cubicle. "I bet you do."

Richard did his best to ignore him. Him, and the chill that shivered down his spine. It wouldn't do any good. McClaine was like a Jack Russell with an old sock whenever he got the sense he was getting under someone's skin. And that was all he had, a scent, an inkling. Just a hunch. He didn't, couldn't know.

He was waiting for him to bite. Richard could see the mirth dancing in his eyes and knew it would be a mistake. So instead, he turned back to his computer. The screen was asleep, but a quick nudge of the mouse brought it alive. Prompted by a security box, he entered his password then watched the various excel spreadsheets pop back up. He bit back a groan. Would it have been too much to ask for a computer virus, or maybe just a good old power cut?

The Prometheus Account.

It had been due well over a week ago, and Scarlet had been on at him to get it done and on her desk by the end of the day.

He'd been working on it all morning, but with everything that had happened, his head just wasn't in the right place. And all the while, Mark had watched him, grinning that inane, shit-eating grin. Just the prospect of a long afternoon of it all over again had him blindly reaching out for his mug of tea. It was cold as ice, but he didn't care.

McClaine cocked a brow. "Ya know that tea's been sitting there all morning, right?"

"Mhm..." Richard murmured, chugging it down, not even tasting it as the memory of Rebecca purring his name in that hot wanton tone burned his ears.

Mr Martin…

"I flushed my pen out in it while you were in the land of nod."

"Mhh-" Eyes widening as the words and the acrid ink flavour registered, Richard pivoted and retched, spitting out the vile mixture into the waste bin beside the desk. "You… asshole!" Coughing, it took everything he had not to hurl the mug at McClaine. What little of his curse made it through the spluttering, however, was lost in the other man's laughing.

"Hey! Why aren't the pair of you out for lunch? Trying to bugger each other over the desk or something?"

Wiping his mouth with the back of his hand, Richard shot a withering sideways glance at Dave Sing. "Or something."

A third generation English-Nepalese, from the generation who had turned their back on the ancestral beliefs and completely assimilated to western culture, Dave Sing was also tall and thin. Handsome, with almond skin and copper eyes, but jet black that hair that he kept short and spiked. He'd joined the firm shortly after Richard, a fresh-faced graduate from Coventry University. Young and ambitious- Richard liked him well enough. An asset to the team, but in dire need of seasoning.

His own lunch in hand, the office's third resident settled in his own seat and was about to take a bite of a generous beef burger when he got his first close-up look at Richard. The burger dropped into its wrapper. "Geez Rich, you look awful."

"Yeah-"

"Yeah, well, what do you expect?" McClaine cut in, just managing to get control of his guffaw. "Ben Dover here had a wild weekend after the do last week."

"What?" Richard rounded on him, his heart in his throat. No, he couldn't know about Rebecca. There was no way he could know, unless-

"Oh, come on, Dick, don't give us any of that old pony. That look your missus got when she saw old Walrus Face's daughter putting the moves on you. You can't honestly expect us to believe you didn't get a little bit. Alice damn near started fucking you right there in front of everyone."

"Fuck off," Richard warned, but inside he felt the knot his insides had wound loosen. Slightly.

McClaine shot Sing a sly look and added under his breath, as if to keep the man sitting just meters away from hearing, "Pity she didn't. What I wouldn't do to see that fine ass bouncing-"

"*Mike!* I'm warning you," Richard growled. "Shut your fucking hole or the next thing out of your mouth will be your teeth." He emphasised the threat by pushing back from the desk and rising to his feet, the rancour contorting his features into a look of such maleficence it had both Sing and McClaine backing away.

McClaine raised both hands in supplication, his face turning pale. "Woah, Dick, woah. I'm just busting your balls. Okay. Okay? I-I I'm sorry. Jeez… just relax. Relax." He was on his feet and backed round the desk.

Richard watched him go, letting him put a bit more space between them before dropping back into his chair.

All the tension seeming to evaporate from the room at once, and McClaine let go of a deep sigh. "We cool? God, my heart's beating so fast I think you were about to give me a coronary."

"Well, you do deserve it from time to time." Richard kept the bitterness from his tone. McClaine was the sort who needed a slap now and then, and he'd enjoyed the opportunity. No matter what, he loved his wife too much to let that sort of slander pass unchastised, but it wasn't worth settling at work. She'd be the first to tell him that. A man has to do what a man has to do, and the first thing a man had to do was to care for his family. Everything else, including giving mouthy gits a smack in the gob, came later.

"Ouch! That hurt. No, seriously mate, what's with you today? You've been bumbling around here like a zombie high off its head."

"Well, can you blame him?" Sing looked up, his burger already much reduced. "You said it yourself. Scarlet has it pretty wet for him. And you've heard the stories."

"Yeah, but come on, you don't believe all that shit, do you? What would she have to gain?"

"What do you mean, what would she have to gain?" Sing looked incredulous; his speech momentarily dissolved into the singsong accent of the Hindu.

"Why would Scarlet want to sleep with Tommy Cox or that asshole Mike in legal? She's a bird. They don't spread their legs for their underlings. What could they do for her? I mean, she's the big boss's daughter. Why should she shag anyone in the firm? If she wants a promotion, or a pony, all she has to do is ask 'Daddy', and Walrus Face will give his little princess anything she wants."

"Please, that is such misogynistic bullshit. A woman can be every bit as abusive as a man. Haven't you read Disclosure?"

"I saw the film," McClaine cut in, and then his features twisted with a leer. "And I tell you, that Demi Moore can suck my cock any day…"

Richard was only half listening to them. He had heard the stories, too. And like McClaine, usually dismissed them as idle office gossip.

Whatever else she might be, Scarlet was undoubtedly a very beautiful woman, and beautiful women in positions of power and authority attracted rumours the way a dog drew fleas. Often as not, they were just stories spread by jealous colleagues or bitter subordinates left in her wake- and Scarlet wasn't short of those. Quite the reverse in fact, but she was also the daughter of the firm's MD, Derick Holmes. The consequence for any employee caught besmirching her good name would be unpleasant, but after their encounter on Friday, Richard was no longer entirely convinced all the stories were *just* stories, but he wasn't about to admit it.

There'd been a look in her eyes. A certain, predatory gleam…

"Okay, that's enough," Richard snapped. "Have either of you actually spoken to anyone who actually fucked her? Or heard a story that wasn't from a guy who spoke to a guy?"

McClaine's grin dropped. "No."

"Well no," Sing admitted, shoving the empty burger box into a desk drawer. "But Jasper Hawkins told me he once saw her going down on the girl from the mailroom." He looked vindicated.

Until McClaine asked, "Umm, Davey-boy, remind me, what happened to Jasper Hawkins?"

Sing shrugged. "Walrus Face kicked him to the curb."

"For?"

"Improper conduct."

Richard barked a triumphant laugh. "Ha! Exactly, telling tales about his daughter. See, he was talking out of his arse and got canned for it. So, with that cleared up, can we get off this subject? I don't fancy getting sued for libel."

"Slander," Sing corrected.

"What?"

"Libel's written. You mean you don't fancy getting sued for slander."

Richard gave him the finger. "Oh, shut it Apu. I don't give a damn. If you have to be so pedantic, why don't you take a look at this," he scooted back, making room for the pair. Sing and McClaine exchanged a look, then pushed back from their own desks and walked around to his. "I told Scarlet I'd get this report over to her this morning, but the numbers don't add up. I don't know. Is there something I'm not seeing?"

"So?" McClaine asked, coming up to peer over Richard's shoulder. "You know the drill. If it doesn't add up, just attach an advisory."

Sing nodded in agreement. "That's company policy."

Hemmed in by the tight confines of the one-person cubicle, Richard felt the room growing noticeably stuffier. "I know, but something just doesn't feel right."

"Geez, Dick!" McClaine exclaimed, slapping a hand down on the desk. "Why are you making this so hard for yourself? You know the bitch has a major stick up her ass about this sort of thing. Just give her the report. It's not your job anymore-"

"Mr Martin?"

The semi that had been slowly diminishing surged to renewed life as Richard's heart leapt into his throat, his head snapping up. And then he was back there in that bedroom, naked, with *her* stretched out beneath him, his cock buried to the root in her lush, grasping heat. That sweet voice hot and panting in his ear.

"Ah… ahhh-oh my God-oh my God-oh my God… I can't take it… it's too much… too big!" she shrieked, her fingers clawing at the walls and eyes wide with pure ecstasy. "Oh yes… yes… don't stop… I'm all yours Mr Martin… I've wanted your hard cock inside me for so long… you can fuck me whenever you want to… just don't stop… don't stop!"

Rebecca stood in the office doorway.

It was the first he'd seen of the girl since their tryst Friday night, and she looked amazing.

Her white button up blouse was smart and conservative, and while too short to reach her knees, that skirt would have to go a hell of a lot higher to offend any granny's delicate sense of decency, or workplace dress code. Yes, there was nothing overtly sexual in her attire, but the thought of what she hid underneath- those lush full tits, her tight athletic build, made it all sexy as hell. And she was gorgeous, too. Her dark chestnut hair had been tied into its customary side braid and there was a little dusting of blusher to her checks, but it was her lips that caught his eyes first. There was a glossiness to them that immediately made him ache to kiss her, taste her…

She must have come straight from work; it was the only time she wore make-up.

"Hi Rebecca." The words sounded feeble, but it was the best he could do on the spot. Though he'd known this moment would eventually come, he'd been so obsessed with what he'd tell Alice, he'd never actually thought about what to say to Rebecca. "What are you doing here?"

"Mrs Martin called. She thought you might be getting hungry." She beamed a sweet girlish smile and held up a plastic bag. "You forgot your lunch."

"Ah… Thanks… Rebecca," he nodded, feeling suddenly embarrassed. He'd been in such a fluster that morning he'd left his Tesco's pasta salad in the fridge and hadn't noticed until he'd been halfway to work. "Just plonk it down over on that cabinet other there. I'll get to it in a bit. How much do I owe you?"

She beamed, sweeping past him and around the desks. "Don't sweat it, it's on me."

"Really?" He pivoted in his chair to follow her. "You sure about that?"

"Yeah, it's nothing. I wanted to check out the Victorian Market anyway, so it's no big deal." Her smile seemed to broaden. "And I got a *big* bonus over the weekend."

A big bonus? Fuck, what did she mean? Richard felt cold fingers trail down his spine. Was she planning to blackmail him, to keep what happened a secret? He wouldn't have thought so. The girl generally had all the sly cunning of a Care Bear. Then again, she had told Alice, and who had secretly told him, that she'd been saving to move out and get away from her father.

Hush-money could go a long way there.

Or was she after something else?

Something more *physical*.

The prospect made the knot in Richard's gut tighten and he was torn between terror and being a little turned on. "That's cool. Well, thanks Rebecca. I owe you-"

"Urh, Mr Martin, could I have a word with you? Um…"

"Ah, well, now isn't really the best time. You caught us at a bit of a bad moment and-"

"Aw, don't be silly Dick, we can spare the girl a moment," McClaine's eyes glittered darkly as he gave the girl a slow, less than subtle once over.

Rebecca quickly twisted away from his scrutiny. "Er- no! No, I understand." Then she gave Richard a sideways glance, a small smile curling those lush pink lips. "If you want, you could just pop round later… If you have the time that-that is, that is, please, I don't want to put you out and my dad will be out so -"

"Ah… No, that's alright." Remembering her standing at the door in that little black *thing*, Richard swallowed. He couldn't be alone with her, not there. He was safe here. This was his work; she wouldn't try anything here.

And more importantly, nor would he.

He glanced nervously at his co-workers. They were both grinning like a pair of mangy hyenas. "Mind giving us a minute, lads?"

"Sure." McClaine gave Sing a nudge. "Come on Apu, let us leave Dick Hefner here to tend to his little lady friend." However, he paused by the door after the smaller man had gone through and threw a sideways glance back at Richard. "Oh, and enjoy yourself Dick, you're more in need of a blow job than any other white man in history."

Bastard.

Richard cursed and turned away, flipping him the V-Sign over his shoulder. It was an almost impotent retort, but it was the best he could do with Rebecca in such close proximity. He couldn't risk over reacting. He couldn't take the chance of giving his work mate cause to think something was going on.

So he kept his attention locked on his screen, even after the door shut and the laughter drowned out by the hum of computer drives. Yet his eyes had a mind of their own and every few moments he caught himself glancing over in her direction as Rebecca jumped up to perch her ripe little derriere on the edge of his desk, her pencil skirt riding up as she crossed her legs to flash him a hint of thigh.

Thighs that had been wrapped around him just days ago.

Growing ever more aware of the stiffness between his legs, while his guts twisted into knots, Richard swivelled around to face her, blindly tapping a few keys to minimise the spreadsheets. Not that he thought she would have any interest in them, but PPI was such a hot topic, better safe than sorry.

Forcing down a dry swallow, he smiled pleasantly at her. "So, what's so urgent?"

"Well… I wanted to… um it's just that… Well…" She looked away, a blush staining her cheeks a dusty pink. "I'm sorry. About what happened on Friday, I don't know what got into me…"

"I think I have some idea." He couldn't help a dry chuckle.

"I didn't mean like that," Rebecca laughed, the sound high and girlish, breaking the tension that had been building between them.

For a moment.

Then the dam broke, and she started to cry. Fat, glassy tears rolled down her checks in rivers. "I'm so sorry, Mr Martin. I didn't mean for it to happen. Please, please don't hate me. I- I couldn't…"

Her tears raked him. "Hey, hey, hey, come here." Richard opened his arms. She all but threw herself at him, burying her face into his neck and sobbing loudly as he hugged her back. "It's okay, sweetheart. It wasn't your fault. Everything just happened so fast…"

Not sure what else to do, he held her till the tears passed, and then he continued to hold her, rocking gently from side to side. It felt good to hold her like this. She felt good. Her hair was silky soft against his cheek. That lean athlete's build fitting against him so perfectly, warm and so very inviting. Those lush young breasts pushing against his chest through the material of her uniform, tipped by dusky nipples that just begged to be sucked.

"Mr Martin?" Rebecca voiced, her tone shaky and uncertain, and he was suddenly aware she was looking down. Down at where the bulge was pitching a tent in his trousers.

Oh shit…

Heat burned across his cheeks as her head tilted back up to his, those full lips curling into a sly feline smirk.

"H-how was the market?"

No sooner had the words left his mouth, he knew they were a mistake.

Only, he had no idea what else to say. The question was the first thing that came to mind that didn't also involve the words fuck, cunt, cock, tits or cum- in one insidious combination or another.

"Oh... It's amazing!" She positively beamed at the question, her big doe eyes lighting up with mischief. "There are so many stalls this year, and the costumes. It's just like something out of Dickens' times."

"That's... nice. Err Rebecca I have to-"

She carried on regardless. "They've even set up a snow machine over the ice rink..."

"Rebecca-"

"But it's broken and..."

"Rebecca... look... I... I don't think-"

"You should hurry up and eat your sandwich, Mr Martin, before it gets cold."

"Rebecca..." He really needed her to stop talking.

"Mmm... it's pulled pork. I had the hog roast sausage. I normally prefer chicken, but when I saw them on the spit, I couldn't resist. They were just so big and thick; I wasn't even sure I could get it in my mouth-"

He took her mouth, kissing her hard and hungrily, drinking in her lushness.

It was madness. Utter madness. But Richard couldn't take it. He had to have her again. Pulling her into his lap, his hands slid down the lines of her narrow waist to cup and squeeze her butt through her skirt, crushing her to him, making her moan and arch. Fuck, she tasted even better than he remembered. There was no trace of cherries now. Only the lushness of her soft pink lips, and she was all the sweeter for it.

Rebecca didn't waste a moment. Burying her hands in his hair, she sucked his tongue like a woman possessed and moaned a low purr that vibrated through him and made his trapped cock throb against its confines.

Yet it wasn't enough. Nowhere near enough. He wanted more. He wanted her, wanted to rip her shirt open and taste those plump tits. Wanted to bury his face between her legs and eat her hot, wet cunt. Wanted to bend her over his desk, go balls deep in that tempting little pussy and fuck her like the hot little bitch she was.

She moaned a pitiful protest when he left her mouth, but it quickly turned to small kittenish gasps as he nipped a fiery trail down the long slope of her neck. Then she was like putty in his hands. Her hands dropped down to push his jacket halfway down his arms, before working on his shirt buttons, fumbling a bit as he sucked the sweet spot where her neck and shoulder met.

"Oh… Mr Martin!" Rebecca moaned, her head rolling back, exposing more skin for him to kiss. He greedily obliged, dragging the flat of his tongue along the dips and hollows of her throat. Meanwhile, his hands ground her on the ridge of his cock, sliding under the hem of her skirt and up to the warmth beneath. Up along the smooth, silky-soft skin of her inner thigh. Fingers stretching, brushing over taught tendons and reaching for the heat of her lush wet-

A door slammed shut somewhere down the hall, and Richard's heart leaped into his throat. He froze, a moment of clarity rushing over him in an icy cascade.

Shit!

"Stop. Stop- shh!" Seizing Rebecca's arms, he pushed her away, quite literally holding her at an arm's length as he threw a sideways look towards the door.

It was still shut, but the window would have given anyone passing by a front-row seat of their own dirty little peep show.

He watched it, not daring to blink.

Ten seconds.

Thirty seconds.

One minute and still nothing.

He let out a breath. That was close. He didn't want to think what might have happened if someone had seen them. Even now, with their flushed faces and dishevelled condition, it wouldn't have taken Doctor-bleeding-Spock to work out what had been going on.

"Mr Martin?"

Rebecca's voice was so quiet and unsure, it was almost a stranger's voice. He twisted back to face her, and the look in her eyes raked his soul. She couldn't have looked more hurt if he had slapped her.

"Rebecca…" The words caught in his throat. He'd seriously fucked up. Again. "We can't do this."

"Why not?"

Richard felt like the lowest piece of shit that had ever walked the earth. "You know why. I'm married, and I love my wife."

"She doesn't have to know."

"That's not the point. Alice deserves better than that, and so do you." Unable to look her in the eyes, he shrugged his jacket back into place before fixing his buttons. "I don't want to use you like that, Rebecca."

"I don't care. You can use me however you want. I-"

The sudden shrill shriek of a phone ringing cut her off. His computer monitor burst into life, and Alice's face stared back at them.

Chapter Three

"Get down," Richard snapped, not exactly pushing the girl away but urging her off of his lap and down under the desk with an insistence that brokered no argument from her. Then, heart pounding like a drum in his chest, he turned back to the screen.

The Skype video call was getting close to timing out.

Resisting the urge to glance down to the girl's hideaway, he accepted the video call, then forced a broad smile. "Hey Al."

His wife's avatar minimised, and Alice's smoky gaze met his.

"Not interrupting anything, am I, *Dick?*" Even wrapped around an insinuation, her husky tone made his dick hard all over again.

Or maybe it was just the sight of her all dressed up in her '*work wear*'. No doubt, the sight of Alice in that tan blazer, button up blouse, and white pencil skirt had fuelled more than a few teenage boys to lock themselves in the toilets for an extended break.

"Nah, just taking my break. How's work?"

"Boring," she pouted. "I seem to spend all day either marking half-term homework or giving out detentions... Errr, I hate November."

"Aww... don't worry, love, it'll soon be Christmas."

She rolled her eyes. "Ha... ha... ha... Don't remind me."

Alice loved her work. She loved being a teacher, but there were times when the job didn't love her. "Speaking of Christmas, you left your lunch at home, so I gave Rebecca a call and asked her to pop in with something special for you."

Her tone was playful, but the edge to her voice sent a shiver down his spine, and he found himself glancing down at the dark space under his desk.

"Yeah... she just left." He picked up his still wrapped sandwich and held it up for her to see.

A ghost of a smile curved the corner of her mouth and the tip of her tongue darted out across her plump upper lip. "Mmm... good, because I have a little surprise for you."

Momentarily lost in all the memories of just what that tongue and mouth could do, Richard could only swallow. "Oh..."

She leaned back in her big black chair and began working on the buttons of her blouse. "I admit I was rather miffed with you over the weekend for getting in so late the other night, but I think I know a way for you to make it up to me..."

Richard couldn't believe his eyes. "Jesus, Alice... are you mad?"

"Come on *Dick*, I don't have long till my next class... mmm... one of my students might come by at any minute..." As the last button came undone, the blouse fell open to tease him with a glimpse of her breasts, full and firm and absolutely luscious, before she pressed it closed. "Whoopsie..."

"Tease."

"Aww... remember how we used to do this whenever one of us was working late... come on baby..." She let one corner of the garment slide down to reveal her left breast before cupping it. "Mmm... you like these baby, God I wish you were here... I'm so horny... I just want to jerk your big dick off with my tits and watch you paint them with all your yummy cum..."

Richard had to force himself to breathe as he watched his wife raise her tit up to her mouth and swirl her tongue around the pebbled nipple. She knew how much he loved her tits. Knew just how to use them to drive him wild.

"A-Alice..."

"Do you want me to beg for it... want me to get down on my hands and knees... and beg to see your cock..." The blouse fell open completely as Alice pushed her breasts together, making them bounce and jiggle before rolling the dusky nipples between her fingers and thumbs. "Mmm... you're so bad. Do it, Dick, I want your cock."

And his cock definitely wanted her.

That throaty husk of hers had him as hard as steel.

Sensation rippled up and down his length as it fought to be free of its restraints. So insistent and demanding, his white knuckled grip on the armrests of his chair was all that kept him from ripping open his chinos and giving her the show she craved.

Then he felt something brush against his leg.

He froze.

He knew he shouldn't look, but his eyes had a will of their own. Drawn down like magnets to watch the slow seduction of a hand rising from under the desk. Slowly, step by step, walking up his leg bit by bit towards the bulge of his cock, getting closer and closer and…

"*Fuck*…" A ragged breath left him in a rush as soft digits curled around his imprisoned length and gave it a testing squeeze.

"That's it, grab it baby, tell me how big it is… so big and hard and full of cum…" Alice panted in her hot breathy tone, the fingers of her left hand roughly attending to her nipple, twisting and tugging in the way that always got her hot. "Just thinking about you sitting there, jerking your big dick for me… mmm… gets me so wet. Does it feel good, Dick?"

"Yeah… so fucking good…" Richard groaned, Rebecca's small hand fisting him through his trousers, pumping along his length from root to head, her movements slow but urgent. He tried to focus on the screen, on his wife, to blot out the sensations Rebecca was sending sizzling through him, but he was too finitely aware of her. Aware of her shuffling closer, her head of dark chocolate hair creeping out from beneath the table, her free hand creeping up his other leg. Moving higher and higher towards his zipper.

He needed to stop this. He needed to stop her, but when he tried, his body had a will of its own. Instead of pushing her away, his hands just undid the fastenings of his belt and trousers. Then Rebecca's hand was dragging him from the confines of his boxers, and it was too late.

"Suck it." The command was out before he knew what he was saying.

"Fuck yes, baby, I love sucking your cock..." Alice moaned on the screen, thinking the command was for her. "I really wish you were here. Your cock's so big and tasty. I could suck it all day, jerking you off with my tits until you paint my face with your cum. Or would you just bend me over and pound-pound me... pound me from behind..."

She was getting close; he could hear it in her voice. Richard could imagine her hand under the desk, fingers pushing under the silk of her panties to rub her clit. "Stick it in me Dick. I need it. I've been such a naughty schoolgirl, bend me over your desk and punish me... punish me with it... spank my ass with your cock and use my naughty little pussy... she's so nice and hot and wet for you... just begging to get your dick off- oh shit!"

Through the speakers, the school bell sounded faint and distant, but it hit Alice like ice.

In a flash, she was up and pulling herself together as the hall outside filled with the shouts and bangs of children running to their next class. "Sorry babe, gotta go, but we'll finish this later," she promised, before killing the Skype connection with a click of her mouse.

Richard hardly noticed.

Instead, his eyes never strayed from the vision of Rebecca's big doe eyes staring up at him from beneath her bangs as her pink lips wrapped around his cock. A picture of innocence and wickedness. Then she was taking him in. Those lush lips brushing over his glands and down his shaft. The wet heat of her mouth enveloped him, sucking him in all the way to the gate of her throat, before pulling back to mouth his sensitive crown.

"You've no idea how long I've wanted to do this, Mr Martin," she purred, teasing his underside with slow licks. "I'm sorry, I know it's wrong, but after Friday night, I just can't help myself…"

"It's okay Rebecca, that wasn't… it-it's not your fault."

Richard groaned, his head rolling back as the hand still holding him began pumping up and down.

"It's alright, Mr Martin. I know you're only saying that. It's all my fault. I'm such a naughty girl, going down on you while you're talking to your wife. Have I been bad, Mr Martin?"

"Yeah, so very bad."

"Do you like it Mr Martin?

"*Yes.*" The feeling was so intense that Richard's death grip almost snapped the arms clean off his chair.

"Are you going to punish me?"

"Oh yes, I'm going to put you over my knee alright, and if you don't make me cum quickly, I'll bend you over and fuck you across this desk until you can't walk straight."

"Oh, promises, promises…"

She took him back into her mouth. Her cheeks hollowed as she sucked hard, head bobbing up and down while fisting his root, making up whatever she lacked in experience with enthusiasm.

"Mmm... yes, yes, yes... just like that..." Richard groaned, almost as much for her benefit as for his, the words just tumbling out as he melted back into his chair. His hands lost themselves in the silky softness of her hair. He gathered up and pushed back a wing of dark chocolate that had fallen out of place, before fisting it as the flat of her tongue swirled around his crest once, twice, thri- *oh fuck!*

The sensation came upon him so quickly, he didn't have a chance to voice a warning before his hot cum fired into her greedy mouth. His orgasm ripped through him hard enough for black spots to dance before his eyes, but Rebecca accepted everything he had to give her.

She drank every drop. Swallowing greedily as it flowed, sucking when the tide ebbed. And all the while watching him, those big doe eyes bright with... what?

Satisfaction at having brought him to orgasm so easily?

Or excitement about future possibilities?

Only when she had finally milked him dry and his fingers slipped from her hair did she release his still firm erection and stand back up. Taking the napkin from the uneaten sandwich, she wiped her lovely rosy lips clean. Stepping around his chair, she lent down and pressed a soft kiss to his cheek.

"I better get back. See you later, Mr Martin."

"Rebecca wait-" Richard started, but her cute little derriere was already sashaying out the office, the door slamming shut behind her.

His fist hit the desk, hard enough to make the structure tremble. "Shit!"

You stupid bloody bastard, he cursed inwardly as guilt and shame raked him with claws of ice and fire, respawning the sicking knot deep in his guts. How the fuck could he have been so stupid to have let that happen, again?

A ping sounded from the computer, making Richard's heart leap into his throat. His head snapped up to see the icon for the unfinished report flash. The ping was a pre-programed reminder to warn the user whenever a file had been open and inactive for too long.

Richard contemplated it for a second. "Fuck it!"

Tapping a few keys, he deleted his notes, closed the document and forwarded it in an email to Scarlet's inbox.

They were right. It wasn't his job anymore. What the fuck did it matter, anyway?

Shoving himself into his trousers and refastening his belt, he grabbed his untouched sandwich and took a bite.

Only, he'd lost his appetite.

Chapter Four

"We're heading off, Dick. Catch you later."

Richard looked up from his monitor just in time to glimpse McClaine and Sing trot out the office with backhanded waves, like schoolboys ditching detention. "You guys off already?"

"*Already?* Do me a favour, Dick, take a day off, will ya."

"Go see the girls at Spearmint Rhino. They do your sort of favours, mate, not me."

McClaine shot him a look that could curdle custard, then raised his hand, pulled back his cuff and pointed to his TAG Heuer watch face. "See this? It's past five. That's clocking off time in my book. You might be prepared to work yourself ragged, but I've got better things to do than kill myself for old Walrus Face and little miss Tight Ass. Some of us have a life, ya know, see ya."

"You live with your mother!" Resisting the urge to flip him the finger, Richard turned back to his desk, his eyes landing on a mountain of paperwork. Work he'd been putting off while obsessing over the Prometheus Account.

He checked his own wristwatch, a Seiko his old man had given him for his eighteenth birthday. Sure enough, it was five thirteen in the afternoon. He'd been at it for five hours, five bloody hours, and hadn't even made a dent.

Bugger.

Exhaling a long, suddenly exhausted breath, he reclined back in his seat and pushed a hand through his hair. He supposed he should follow their lead and go home. This work could wait a night, and Alice would be on her way home soon enough, after she'd picked up Alex from her parents and battled her way up the stretch of M5 that connected Bristol and Gloucester, through the last of the rush hour traffic. They'd have a nice family dinner before sitting down to… what? Talk about their day?

That's good darling. My day? It was ok. I struggled a bit with that report, but Rebecca gave me a blowjob when she popped by. So all in all…

The thought had a dry laugh billowing up his throat.

How could he look Alice in the eyes again? Hold their son again?

No, he couldn't. Not now, not after…

The computer emitted a small double ring and an email notification window popped up in the bottom right-hand corner of the screen. It was from Scarlet, though the address attached read *Tight_Ass_Bitch.*

Officially, no one knew who had hacked her email to change the address. Whoever it was though, their joke had backfired. Far from being annoyed or embarrassed by the stunt, Scarlet practically adopted the title, and never missed an opportunity to live up to it.

True to her unofficial title, the message was brief and to the point.

> *Dick*
> *Drop by my office on your way out.*
> *We need to discuss Prometheus.*
> *Scarlet*

"… Shit," Richard cursed and looked mournfully back to the paperwork and the potential overtime it offered. "Well, that puts the kibosh on that plan."

He closed the mail with a click of his mouse.

The door was sleek pine with a bronze plaque embossed with the legend, *S. Holmes, Accounts Supervisor*.

Being the boss's daughter certainly had its perks.

Richard knocked once, then pushed on through without waiting for an answer.

Seated at the immense leather-topped oak desk that dwarfed her and the rest of the office, Scarlet was working on her computer. Behind her, floor to ceiling windows boasted a picturesque landscape of the river below.

To a stranger, she might have looked oblivious, blind to the goings on around her, her focus dominated by her work, but Richard knew better. Scarlet was anything but oblivious. She was the sort of woman who woke up intending to conquer the world. Who missed nothing.

Without waiting for an invitation, he crossed the wood panelled floor, bypassing the plush leather sofa to take the simple leather and teak chair opposite her side of the desk.

She didn't look up, nod, or do anything to acknowledge his presence.

Nor would she. Not yet. Not until she was ready.

It was her game, a power play to remind the minion just who was the boss.

Well, at least she didn't make him pass her tea or pick pens off of the floor.

The office had been the department's briefing room before her appointment. Her predecessor had made do with the windowless coat cupboard three doors down. It was simple and functional, but large enough to impress. And beige. Very beige. Beige walls. Beige rugs. Beige leather…

Beige. Safe and soothing, and not at all Scarlet Holmes.

She was as bloody crimson as her namesake. And then a dash extra.

All heat and passion and searing raw emotion. And beauty.

Scarlet flaunted flawless skin, tanned to a soft peach hue, that complimented the waves of spun gold that tumbled down to her shoulders. She wore a tight white dress that showed off plenty of leg and had a deep plunging neckline to emphasise her figure. There wasn't a man alive who could deny Scarlet was *very* lovely.

The matter wasn't up for discussion. It was a fact.

And only skin deep.

Beneath the fragile beauty, she was as hard and sharp as steel. A lioness disguised in a little bunny's fur.

He ignored the urge to check his watch. That subtle hint would only prolong the game, though. Scarlet would see to that, sure enough. So instead, he amused himself by watching the goings on outside the tall windows behind her desk that overlooked the line of narrow boats and yachts moored along the Sharpness Canal.

The view was wasted on Scarlet.

When she turned to him, the bunny beamed up at him. "Hey Dick."

"Hi Scarlet," Richard smiled back, inwardly steeling himself. If she wanted to play her games, he'd play. "How was your day?"

It was a poor effort, but the best he could do on the fly. It got the job done.

"Oh, the usual, same shit, different day. You headin' home for the day?"

"Yeah soon, just had a couple of things I wanted to finish up first."

She ignored the prompt and just kept smiling up at him.

Sod it, she could have this round. "So, you wanted to see me?"

Her eyes were bright, and they laughed at him behind her glasses. She didn't need them. The lenses were from a cheap pair of reading glasses she'd got in a Pound shop, but the frames were designer and worth more than he made in a month. "Yes, we need to discuss Prometheus."

"Oh? How come?"

"Don't play coy with me, Dick." Despite her smile, behind the cheap plastic lenses, her eyes flared with blue fire. Behind the bunny, the lion was baring its fangs, a warning before the charge. "I told you I wanted you to make the Prometheus Account your top priority, yes?"

"Yes."

"Yes? That was a month ago. The report should have taken you a few days, max. And now you send me this?" She pulled a manilla folder out of a drawer and laid it open on the desk. A quick glance confirmed it was the paperwork he'd sent her earlier. "So, what's the game?"

"Game?"

"You could have knocked this up in a few hours. You have been, all afternoon. So, either you had a hunch, then lost your nerve, or you were slacking off to make me look bad. Which is it?" Closing the folder, she slid it aside, then leaned forward to face him, fingers tipped by perfectly manicured nails painted speckled gold, steepled under her chin.

"Scarlett I…"

"Do you have a problem working under me, Dick?"

"No."

"Then you had a hunch?"

"It was a stupid idea, not worth mentioning."

"You thought it was important enough to risk the contract."

Reaching into his pocket, he pulled out the flash drive with all his research into Prometheus and laid it on the desk. He'd forgotten about it amongst everything else that had gone on in the last couple of days and had only thought of it after receiving her email. He'd brought it along just in case. "It's nothing."

"Why don't you let me be the judge of that." She took the flash drive and plugged it into her desktop. With a few clicks of her mouse, all the documents were arranged on her monitor. Spreadsheets. Invoices. Tax returns. Everything he could find on Prometheus, but would it be enough?

A tight knot of tension wound around and around his guts like a python's coils. Financial reports. Richard watched her work. Those fierce blue eyes skimmed over the screen behind her glasses, moving from one article to the next while she caught her rose-pink lower lip between a perfect set of pearly whites.

He hated to admit it, but her look was sexy as hell.

She swivelled slowly back around in her chair to face him; her stare piercing. Not quite a lioness, but definitely not a flopsy bunny either. "All this shows is Prometheus recorded substantial profits. Hardy conclusive, *Dick*."

A low shiver coursed down his spine to tingle in his crotch as his cock stirred at the way she said his growingly official nickname. The accusation behind it made him feel like he was getting a telling off from the hot teacher all the boys fantasised about.

"Since the early 90s, Prometheus has consistently recorded growing profits. Yes, however, if you look more closely, you'll see the bulk of their earnings came from work throughout Ukraine, Estonia, Georgia, Kazakhstan, and the Baltic states. Nations recovering from the Soviet Union. Plenty of cheap labour, but a brassic economy. Prometheus's books took a slight hit in the Global recession but remained firmly in the black until 2012, when they expanded their operations into the Middle East. Work in areas of Turkey and Syria achieved record profits, despite the numerous conflicts raging in the region." He paused, trying to think how to put the next part.

"Go on…"

He took a breath, steeling his nerves for the plunge. "I think Prometheus has connections with Russian organised crime and is a front for criminal activity, including money laundering, drug trafficking and smuggling."

And there it was, the complete ruin of his career. And all packed up neatly in one sentence. Who says experience counts for nothing!

For the longest moment, Scarlet let the silence drag on. Her expression impassive, unreadable, neither bunny nor lion, but her eyes, once such a vibrant blue, were suddenly steel. "I see." Her tone was as cold and sharp as ice. "Those are very serious accusations, Dick. Ones we're required by law to report to the proper authorities and would almost certainly result in us losing the client, even if you're wrong. Can you prove this?"

"No," he confessed, then added hastily. "But there are too many anomalies for it all to be just coincidence."

"What anomalies?"

"The company was founded in the early 90s and received heavy outside funding, primarily from a now disbanded Russian-led consortium, at the same time Russian gangsters started moving west out of Moscow. They do business all over Europe but are especially affluent in areas of high Russian criminal activity and interest."

Scarlet nodded. "And their 2012 expansion?"

"The date they began expanding was just a month after the Russian President's second inauguration. It's not exactly a secret he uses the crime bosses as off the book enforcers, and the countries Prometheus has expanded to have seen heavy Russian influence since."

"They're war zones, Dick," she laughed without mirth, shaking her head. "Builders and developers often receive government contracts to repair and rebuild sites damaged in conflict."

"Yes, but usually after the war is won," Richard cut in. "I've heard of prudent planning, but if I'm wrong, whoever picked these deals must have one hell of a crystal ball. You should take him to the Cheltenham races next year. With this guy's luck, you'll make a fortune betting on the gee-gees."

She ignored the joke, instead turning back to look over the documents on her screen. "Well, the money laundering is self-explanatory. Dirty money finances the projects on the books, then returns as profits, but what about this trafficking and smuggling nonsense?"

What? Was she actually buying this story? He couldn't believe it; he'd half expected her to tear up his contract right there, even for suggesting it.

"They ship out their own equipment instead of hiring or purchasing on-site. A JCB is a pretty big bit of kit. Lots of places to hide something you don't want found, if you know how."

"But you can't prove it. Legally."

"No." His throat was so tight, he had to force the word out. "After tax is accounted for, their profits are all funnelled into an account in a private Depository Bank in Zurich. I can't track it from there without going through a long and costly legal battle."

"So…" she rounded on him, her voice as cold and sharp as steel. "Let me get this straight, because I'm a little confused. You're given a high value contract, told to make them your top priority, but instead of doing your job and having the report on my desk like you're supposed to, you dig into their business records and concoct some cock and bull theory about the Russian Mafia. And just to put the icing on the cake, you have no proof? Nothing to back it up. Is that about the sum of it?"

"More or less."

She sighed and shook her head.

That was it. She'd just fired her broadside and hit dead centre. He was sunk. He might as well go back and clear out his desk. Save the trip in tomorrow and have a lie in-

"Why did you keep digging? Why not just hand it in when you were supposed to after hitting a dead end?"

Richard had to work hard to keep his confusion from showing.

Why had he kept digging? Force of habit? Professional curiosity? His last job had done checks all the time, and he'd never let it go on for so long. There had just been something. Something not right. Something he couldn't put his finger on. Just something. Just…

"Just a hunch."

"A hunch?" She leaned back in her chair. "Well Dick, I don't know what to say, except…" Her full red lips spread into a wide smile, with just the hint of a white lion's fang. "Congratulations."

Chapter Five

Richard blinked, almost at a loss for words. Almost.

Congratulations? For what? Dropping a bollock? Making a complete ass of himself? "What?"

Scarlet's head titled, her eyes dancing and gleeful, both bunny and lioness. "Congratulations. You passed the test."

"Test? What test?" he demanded, incredulous.

"For the position of Financial Analyst," she said simply. "You applied for the position before being assigned to this department."

"Yeah, I remember."

How could he not?

It had been one of the few jobs he'd actually wanted. Similar seniority to his old role, but with a better salary and abundant career opportunities.

Or so the ad in the job centre had led him to believe.

What they'd offered was a polite brush off, followed by a role that was a major move down, with less pay, more hours and with every opportunity he could ever have hoped for, to kiss ass and get his ass kicked. However, with little Alex on the way, what choice had he had? It wasn't like he was getting headhunted by the Bank of England, after all.

"But that was over a year ago." he added, only just able to keep the bite from his tone.

Scarlet nodded, leaning back in her chair. The bunny had taken flight now. She was all lioness here, a queen in the heart of her territory, mistress of all she surveyed, and those hot, ice-blue eyes watched him keenly over her steepled fingers. "As you are aware, the role requires certain aptitudes. Qualities that are difficult to assess on a CV and in an interview. So, potential applicants are allocated a minor role in the company, then in due course, we allocate them a manufactured account to evaluate their performance."

"Hence Prometheus," Richard nodded, comprehension blooming. "Who seduced Zeus with plates of bones wrapped in fats to give offal covered beef to humanity."

"Then stole fire, and was punished by being chained to a rock for the great eagle to feast upon his liver each morning," Scarlet added.

"Very symbolic. So, if the candidate lacks the predisposition for the role, they're fed to the eagles?"

"More or less," she purred with a subtle tilt of her head that made Richard wonder if she wasn't entirely joking. "But, congratulations Dick, you've passed the test. Though I have to say, you were taking your sweet time about it. I was about ready to chuck your ass to the curb on general principle. Rather ironic, really. If you hadn't, you certainly would have been after I read what you sent me earlier. How long did all this take you?"

"About a day and a half," he shrugged, feeling very warm in his suit. It all made so much sense and was now so obvious. God, how could he have been so stupid? Russian organised crime. He must have lost his mind.

"Extraordinary. That's half as long as the last guy who passed the test." Shifting back in her chair and crossing her legs, revealing a lot of her soft, golden thigh, Scarlet brought a hand up to toy with a lock of her hair, studying him with renewed interest. "I must say, though, yours is certainly the most unique report yet. And all from the financial data you were provided and a bit of digging. Just extraordinary. You certainly have a vivid imagination for an accountant, Dick. You've been reading too much Andy McNab. Still, I might just have to commission you to write a novel." The corner of her mouth curled in the ghost of a smile and the tip of her pink tongue swept over her plump, juicy, pink lips. "A seedy little erotic thriller. Perhaps about a businessman caught cheating on his wife."

She let the suggestion hang there, but held his gaze just long enough for Richard's blood to turn to ice in his veins.

Shit.

Was it just a coincidence? Or did Scarlet know something? No, that was crazy. How could she? He was being silly. She couldn't know anything about him and Rebecca, unless- the sound he'd heard outside the office door. Someone moving around behind the door... Had it been Scarlet? Fuck.

"So... I'm getting promoted?"

Smooth, very smooth, asshole.

Whatever Scarlet had been expecting, that wasn't it.

She laughed.

She actually laughed. A soft, kittenish, and unmistakably feminine sound, as fair to the ears as she was lovely to behold. It was the first time Richard had ever heard it and despite his rather precarious situation; it surprised him to find the sweet melody suited her and made her appear more delicate.

He almost forgot what a bitch she could be.

Almost.

"Not quite," she chuckled. "Consider it more of a lateral move. You'll remain in my department, but within a role more suited to your talents. Get a nice little pay raise, your own private office three doors down the hall. Just what you need, a little *privacy...*"

"Is that a prerequisite for the position?" Richard asked, his throat growing tighter.

She giggled softly. "In your case, Dick, I think it's indispensable."

She was baiting him, daring him to ask the question. Both manoeuvring and mocking him. Just another game. Fuck, fuck, fuck!

"If you say so," he said simply, sidestepping her trap by the skin of his teeth. *Great, now all I've got to do is get the hell out of Dodge.*

He just needed an excuse.

Just one polite reason to-

Scarlet's lips twisted wryly. "Very good Dick, but as much as I'd like to sit here engaging in a bit of witty repartee with you, I don't have the time and you don't have the wit, so why don't we just cut through the bullshit." She removed her glasses and placed them on the desk before turning her computer monitor around for him to see.

Oh shit…

A video file was open on the screen, paused for the moment, but Richard recognised it as the feed from a security camera, a camera from his office. The camera that just so happened to be looking down at his cubicle. Where he was sitting… with Rebecca in his lap.

How could he have forgotten about the damn cameras?

Scarlet clicked her tongue, the lioness's merciless blue eyes fixed on him. "Now Dick, I don't care what my staff get up to on their lunch. Frankly, if you're off the clock, I don't give a fuck… so long as it takes place off company property."

She clicked her mouse, and the feed started replaying the scene. There was no sound. The audio was redirected to a pair of buds in the jack, but then again, he didn't need it. Every moment was still seared in his memory. Him and Rebecca making out in his chair. The call from Alice. Rebecca hiding. His wife stripping on the screen while the girl sucked him off… Richard hated to admit it, but even under her scrutiny, the memory of it was making him hard.

"Off the record, I have to say, I'm impressed. I thought the pair of you were just a boring, straight-laced, middle-class couple. The sort that argues twice a week and fucks once every leap year. I certainly never would have guessed Alice had it in her. I mean, I always suspected she had a bit of a wild streak in her. All these stuck-up bitches do, but to actually Skype her man at work to have phone sex! Bravo. And as for you..." She shut down the media player and twisted the monitor back around to face her, her eyes bright and mocking. "Well, look at the cock on you. And while a hot bit of young ass blows you under the desk, as well. Never knew you had it in you, either. I thought that only happened in bad porn."

With a shudder of self-loathing at his treacherous loins, Richard met Scarlet's gaze. "And I never guessed you were such a voyeur. What do you do, sit around here watching us all day?"

"No, not unless I have due cause to check the feeds. And when I spotted your little friend going into one of my departments, then strutting by my office door with that 'cat that got the canary grin' on her face nearly half an hour later... Well, it wouldn't be very professional of me to just turn a blind eye. Who knew what she was getting up to, or rather, who was getting into her..." she chuckled mockingly. "You should thank me, Dick. If someone in security had seen this. Well, who knows how far it could have gone..." She let the point hang there to let his imagination do the rest.

"Is that what happened to you? Did one guard catch you having a bonk and run off to tell Daddy?" The words were out before he could stop himself.

"Excuse me?"

Shit, now he'd done it.

He gritted his teeth against another outburst and tried to look contrite. "Never mind, I-"

"No, go on, *Dick*," she said, raising a hand to stop him, her voice suddenly very still and deadly serious. "So just what are they all saying about me? I'm the office slut? A hot fuck in the closet, or a quick suck in the bog type of girl? Or is it the old chestnut, daddy issues? Sleeping with all of Daddy's little minions because old Walrus Face wouldn't buy her a pony for her tenth birthday?"

"No one said anything about a pony," he admitted, resisting the urge to look away as a chill crept up his spine and he had the unmistakable feeling of shrinking into his chair.

"Then you've missed some of the more lurid variations," she continued. "No Dick, I've never been caught on camera. I'm not a slut, *Dick*. I just like sex and I'm not afraid to show it. Or enjoy it."

Richard wondered for a moment if he should ask, but she spoke with such resolve, he couldn't help himself. "And the stories about you with Tommy Cox, and Mike from Legal."

She shrugged. "They're true. I found them attractive and thought they would be a decent lay. So, I offered, and they took me up on it. They were under no obligations."

Richard was aghast. "They lost their jobs and their wives divorced them because of your affairs. Doesn't that bother you?"

"No!" Scarlet held up a dismissive hand. "Their wives divorced them because they found out their husbands were getting some on the side and didn't like it. And I sacked them because they thought banging the boss's daughter whenever she needed to take the edge off gave them the right to talk shit about the company.

Clearly, they were wrong. If their wives had sucked their dicks once in a while, maybe they would've gone home to them instead of meeting me in the Travel Lodge. So, what do I have to feel guilty about Dick? I'm not married and I'm not lying to my spouse to bang a hot bit of ass." Her smile dropped, and her expression was suddenly as cold and hard as a diamond. "It's rather hypocritical, don't you think, questioning my morals when you're the one getting a little lip service from your bit on the side?"

She had it right, of course. And whatever else his faults might have been, Richard wasn't so great a fool as to try lying to himself.

What right did he have to criticize her?

They may have both been indiscreet, but she was single and a free agent.

He, on the other hand, was a married man.

"Yes. You're right, I'm sorry, and it won't happen again," he capitulated and finally looked down at his feet, running a hand through his hair. Scarlet nodded, accepting his apologies, but it wasn't enough. He felt the need to say more, to explain himself, or perhaps just get it all out in the open. "This all started Friday night, after we got home from the party, and I let myself get carried away in the moment. I made a mistake and now- "

"Why?"

"What?" The question was so unexpected, he rounded on her without thinking.

Yet Scarlet merely looked back, nonplussed. Then, as if he hadn't spoken at all, she calmly pulled open one of her drawers and pulled out a Tupperware tub and a small packet of chocolate dip. "Do you mind? I had lunch but seem to have missed dessert, courtesy of your little show."

He nodded, but without waiting for his response, Scarlet had already stood up and was walking around the desk to sit on the edge directly in front of his chair. She crossed her legs. "So, why was it a mistake?"

"You have got to be joking," he stammered, all too aware of their closeness as the floral scent of her perfume fogged his senses.

"Am I laughing?" she asked, undoing the container's fastenings before carefully balancing the lid on her knee like a plate, then tipping a variable punnet of fat red strawberries out onto it. "If I were joking, Dick, you would be in stitches. Now, this girl-"

"Rebecca," he cut in, perhaps a little too forcefully, but he didn't care. He didn't want her referring to Rebecca in that way. Like she was insignificant.

Scarlet shot him a withering, almost pitying look as she ripped the lid off of her dip. "Okay, *Rebecca*. You've known her a while?"

Richard nodded. "Yeah, she lives in our building. She's our babysitter."

She exaggerated rolling her eyes, then plucked up one strawberry and plunged it in the dip. "I never would have guessed, still I suppose a cliché is a cliché for a reason. Okay, so you've known her a while. And she comes from a troubled home?"

"Y-you could say that," he trailed off for a second as he watched her bring the fruit up to her lips, her tongue sliding out to taste the chocolate. He forced himself to look away, his eyes quickly fixing on a point out the window. There wasn't anywhere else he could look. Her perch on the desk caused the already tiny skirt to rise higher while placing the swells of her breasts just at his eye level…

"Abuse?"

"Something like that. Her old man isn't much cop with men, but he can be a hard one with women."

"You sound like you don't like him." She bit down on the berry and moaned a low sound of pleasure that seemed to thrum down his spine, all the way to the base of his cock.

"We've had words." Actually, Richard had caught the little bastard threatening to beat his daughter black and blue after he'd had a few too many, and she'd come home late. So he had explained, from one father to another, that that wasn't any way to treat his daughter.

The guy had gotten the message, at least for a while. However, the sounds from their flat had been growing more and more volatile recently. No doubt he would have to reiterate that little lesson before long.

She popped the rest of the strawberry into her mouth, her tongue skimming out to lick up the single roll of sweetness that was creeping down her chin. "And I suppose her mum just sits there and lets him bully her around?"

"No, her mother buggered off and left her alone with the short-arse, went to live with a boyfriend in Leeds or Bradford or somewhere up North. Rebecca hasn't seen or spoken to her in years."

She pondered that for a moment, before picking up another strawberry and nibbling it thoughtfully. "No other family?"

"None," he swallowed, his mouth and throat growing dry as the office seemed to grow hotter by the second.

"Then I don't see the problem," she declared, then slowly took the whole berry into her mouth. "She seems smart enough, enough not to think you'll leave your wife for her. She's just confused, as most girls her age are. I dare say you're the strongest male role model she's ever had and can't quite work out how she feels about you. Give her a few weeks to work it out, and she'll meet some boy her own age. But if you tell her it was all a mistake, you'll probably just do more harm than good for the poor girl."

"And what about Alice?"

"Do you love her?" She forewent the fruit entirely this time and dipped her finger into the dip.

"Of course I do, but-"

"Would you leave her for this girl or try to lead either of them on?" Scarlet put her chocolate-covered finger into her mouth and sucked it clean with a long slow draw that had Richard's fists clenching in his lap.

"Never," he rasped, his gaze focusing on those pouting pink lips, and for the briefest moment, he wondered what that lush mouth would look like wrapped around his dick.

She shrugged. "Then? What about her? Sex isn't a luxury, Dick. It's a necessity. The body needs it like it needs food and water. If you're not getting any at home, then you need to look for it elsewhere. If having a little on the side gets the urge out of your system, just enjoy the adventure while it lasts."

"Spoken like a woman who's never been married."

Scarlet smirked triumphantly and gestured at him with another plump strawberry. "And who never wants to. Humans aren't monogamous by nature, so why should I be? Just because society demands it? I'm a girl with needs who doesn't like to be tied down, and matrimony is one big leash, Dick, especially when there are so many men out there I haven't tried yet."

She dunked half the berry into the dip. "Besides, what good would telling her do? Cheaters say being honest is the right thing to do, but all they really want is to make themselves feel better about fucking up. She'll be happier not knowing."

"It's still wrong."

"How so? Is it wrong to grab a bite on the way home even though your wife is cooking dinner? No. You're hungry, so you eat. Why should sex be any different?" Her eyes then sparkled with mischief as she nibbled along the chocolate. "If it bothers you so much, just grow a pair and tell her. Or try for a three-way?"

"Now I know you're joking."

"Why not? It would certainly solve all your problems," she teased, stretching out one long graceful leg, the toe of her high-heel shoe, white to match her dress, brushing along his thigh and down his leg. "And it's certainly not adultery if your wife's banging her, too."

"Except Alice would cut my balls off and wear them as earrings," he breathed, forcing himself to look into her eyes, refusing to look down, all too aware of the unobstructed view she was offering him. Sharon Stone couldn't have done it better herself.

Holding his gaze, she leant forward until they were almost nose to nose. "I don't know. From what I saw, she's definitely full of surprises. It's always the up-tight ones that you've got to watch."

"Drop it Scarlet," he warned, gritting his teeth, his dick hard and tight and impossible to ignore.

"Am I right, Dick? I am, aren't I? Yeah, I bet she turns into a little nympho the moment her hair comes down." She dropped the plate of strawberries on the desk and reached out to finger his tie.

"Scarlet… I'm warning you." His throat was tight around the words as his heart pounded in his ears. Shit, he needed to get out of here. She was too close, he couldn't think, couldn't breathe, her damn perfume was fogging his head.

Damnit, why did she have to smell so good…

"Mmm… you know you're cute when you're flustered." She closed the gap, sliding off the desk and onto his lap so the crotch of her dress pressed against his cock through his trousers. "Come on, Dick, don't be greedy. She'll love going down on your little babysitter while you fuck her like a bitch in hea-"

Her taunt died in a surprised gasp as he seized a fistful of her blonde hair.

Chapter Six

"Shut up."

"Dick!" Scarlet hissed. "W-what're you doing?"

"I said, shut your fucking mouth." His voice was low and deathly calm, a cocktail of anger and lust pulsing through him like nitro-glycerine. Richard lurched to his feet, towering over her...

Except Scarlet wasn't a woman to be dominated. She was a fighter.

She'd fought every day of her life. Against her brothers, against peers who thought her beneath them, against subordinates and superiors alike who thought of her as an entitled and a spoiled brat. It was why she had fought so hard to graduate top of her class at Cambridge. Why she had taken this entry-level role in her father's company and would work her way to the very top, rather than just let him marry her off.

She wouldn't be cowed or humbled or let any man take advantage of her.

The moment her feet touched the ground, she pivoted, twisting free of his grip, her arm sweeping out, nails hooked to claw his face. She attacked with all the swiftness and ferocity of a cornered cat.

However, Richard was faster, twisting out of her reach, grabbing her wrist and dragging it around behind her back, forcing her down across the desk. Before she could fully comprehend what just happened, he was leaning over her, caging her there, pinned against the desk, his body deliciously hard beneath his suit.

"Scream, and I'll gag you," he warned, fettering both her wrists in one hand while the other tugged at his tie, loosening the noose.

"You wouldn't dare." Scarlett shot him an angry look over her shoulder, even as the raw emotion in his voice made her knees weak. No man, or woman for that matter, had ever been this way with her. She'd never known getting dominated could be such a turn on.

Who'd of ever guessed he had it in him?

Richard stared her down, his gaze fixed on that pretty little mouth of hers, her luscious lips just the right size and shape for sucking cock. He was sorely tempted to gag her anyway on principle alone, but he had a better idea.

He was sick of all her bullshit, her teasing, her constant shots at Alice. He might have fucked up, possibly ruined his marriage, his life, and be about to fuck up his career a whole lot more, but that didn't give her the right to belittle his wife. This time, she'd gone too far.

It was time to teach the *Tight Ass Bitch* a lesson.

"Wouldn't I?" A dark grin pulled at the corner of his mouth as he pulled the tie over his head and looped it round Scarlet's wrists in a simple slip knot. "You've been a very bad girl, Scarlet. Do you know what I do with bad girls?" He drew back to stand over her, one hand braced against the small of her back, holding her and her wrists down, the other pushing up her skirt, bearing the lush curves of her naked derriere.

"What?" she gasped, shaking, heat and embarrassment crackling through her, making it impossible for her to stay still.

"This." His hand swept down, slapping her right cheek with a loud crack. "I give them a spanking."

Scarlet couldn't help giving a little gasp. It didn't hurt, not really, but the hot sting made her clit pulse within its hood and she twisted against her bonds, trying to give the little bud some much-needed attention. "*Dick*... I'm your boss-ah!"

He smacked her ass again, the left cheek this time, and *harder*.

"No, Scarlet," he growled, trying to ignore the way her lovely derriere, now marred by a pair of red handprints, was wriggling against the bulge of his cock. Damnit, had she noticed? This would all be for nought if she knew she was affecting him too. He reinforced the assertion with another slap that actually made her jump. "You're a bad girl. Say it."

"No." Scarlet shook her head, but when the blow came, the delicious slap of skin meeting skin and the explosion of heat was too much. She bit her lip to hold the moan at bay, but there was no stopping the slickness between her thighs.

"Say it."

Slap!

"I-I…"

Slap!

"Say it!"

Slap!

"I'm a bad girl!" she moaned, the words flowing from her as thick and sweet as honeyed cream. God, why did it have to feel so good?

Richard raised his hand, then held it there. "Again."

"Mmm… I'm a bad, bad girl!" Biting her lower lip, Scarlet chanced a glance back, her eyes pleading, but for what? Mercy, or perhaps another smack.

His hand dropped to brush over her buttocks. She instinctively flinched away from his touch but relaxed when his fingers began kneading her backside, massaging away the heat. "You admit you've been bad?"

"Yes… very… mmm… bad…" Scarlet purred, pushing back against his hand as he made larger and larger circles. She was so turned on, so wet. What was he doing to her? Why was he making her so horny?

"Teasing me. Trying to seduce me. Belittling my wife." His hand slid down between her legs, fingers reaching, feeling, sliding along her wetness, pushing through her grasping heat.

"*Yes!*" Scarlet gasped, her whole world shrinking down to the feeling of his finger filling her, stroking her delicate inner tissues, swirling and stirring her into wild delirium. Greedy for more, she wriggled and circled against his swirling digit, spreading her legs wider, opening for him.

"That's it, you bad girl, and who's the boss now?"

She swallowed, her body clenching around the digit, the tension building inside her. "You are."

"Again," he growled, curling his finger to brush over that patch of rough tissue under her clit while thrumming the bundle of nerves with the pad of his thumb.

Scarlet gasped, her eyes widening as a fog settled over her thoughts. Sensation rippled outward from wherever he touched, only threatening to crash over her, driving her to the brink. Just not over it. It was the sweetest torture, the cruellest ecstasy.

No one had ever done this to her before, made her feel so vulnerable. It was delicious. "You... You're the boss... *Richard!*"

He couldn't remember the last time she'd used his Christian name. And the way she said it, so pleading and desperate, had his lips twisting in a dark grin before he leant down over her to lick the shell of her ear. "Good girl." He withdrew his finger.

Panic flaring inside her, she twisted right and left, trying to grab his hand, but the tie held strong. "No! Don't stop...!" She yelped as he swatted her arse again, the sting dissolving into delicious throbbing pleasure.

"Are you talking back to me? Bad girl," He growled, his tone low and primal, all but tearing at his belted trousers to liberate his cock. Taking himself in hand, he rubbed the crown along her slick, greedy cleft, the tip sliding through her swollen folds to graze her little bundle of nerves, making her shudder and gasp.

"No... please... Sir... mmm... don't stop... feels so good... I..." Panting, her pussy hot and throbbing, begging, no *demanding* more, Scarlet pressed back, circling her hips, desperate to feel him slide inside her, filling her, pounding her.

It did no good. He had her pinned to her desk, caged by his body, hands bound, completely at his mercy, and it only made her burn hotter.

"What? What do you want, Scarlet?"

"Please…" she heard herself beg. Her throat tightened around the word as she turned to look back over her shoulder at *him*.

This couldn't be the man she knew.

Her subordinate, dependable Richard Martin. The quiet, mild-mannered guy who never gave her a second look. That guy was fun to tease and torment, but did nothing for her, despite his thick dark hair, chiselled bone structure and broad build.

This man, who was now almost nose to nose with her, was different. Everything about him excited her. The way he looked at her, handled her, and just completely dominated her.

God, this couldn't be happening. Who was this man? What was he doing to her? She didn't do things like this, never at work, and she was never submissive in sex. She needed control. Her lovers were quiet and submissive, little more than tools for her pleasure, dildos with a pulse. They couldn't make her beg.

Yet this man had. And fuck, why did it feel so good?

"Louder," Richard pressed, enjoying the moment, relishing the turnaround, the power. He loved hearing her like this. So desperate and needy. All her poise and professionalism stripped away to leave just the raging wanton.

She licked her lips, her eyes smouldering, dark with desire. Needing to move, to take some control, she curled her hips, desperate to stroke her clit against his crest and ease the throbbing ache pulsing there. "Please!"

"Please what?" he asked, the deep growl of his tone sending hot shivers through her core as, bending his knees, he lined himself up, the broad tapered head of his cock nestling between her folds. Just one push and he would be buried inside her.

Scarlet couldn't bear it.

"Fuck me... please, fuck me-oh!" Scarlet gasped, her eyes widening and mouth falling open in a long moan as his hips snapped forward, driving in deep. The delicious shock of his cock sliding home rushed over her, making her head spin.

Too deep. Oh God, he's huge. How the hell does Alice ever ride this beast?

"Yeah, is this what you want, Scarlet?" he rasped in a low and sultry voice that just screamed sex. His hands dropped to her hips, fingers squeezing hard enough for her to feel the bite, both dragging her back and tilting her at just the right angle to take him. Not so much holding her as using her body to fuck her back onto his cock.

"Oh yes... oh yes... yes Sir!" she panted, her insides clenching, squeezing all around him, pleasure rippling out to her fingers and toes as she felt herself open to him, inch by sinfully thick, hard inch of him. Fuck, she'd never dreamed someone could fill her so completely. "Oh fuck... oh my God... yes... make me take it. I've been such a horrible boss, I need to be punished… mmm… punish that pussy with your big fucking dick!"

Richard was more than happy to oblige. "Don't worry, you're going to get everything you deserve."

Fuck, what the hell was wrong with him? He didn't dominate his lovers, didn't degrade or overpower them. This wasn't him. He'd never been like this with Alice, hadn't been like it with Rebecca… but he liked it.

"Just look at you, you bad girl. Getting fucked across your desk with your hands tied behind your back. Your snug little cunt milking my cock. You're just bloody loving this, aren't you?"

It was time to teach his boss's daughter a lesson.

She had been asking for this, well now it was time she learned to be careful what she wished for.

"Yes! Yes, I love it!" Scarlet moaned, writhing in his arms as his hips curled against her derriere. There was a momentary feeling of emptiness as he pulled back before his hands snapped her back to meet his hard thrust, making her feel every hard inch of his godly cock driving her up onto her tiptoes.

The feeling was so intense. She felt so stretched. So full.

It made her whole core pulse and tingle, and clench around him, but it was too late. He was already sliding out, almost all the way, then driving into her again, and again, until he was pounding into her greedy sex. "I'm a bad little whore… bad fucking whore… pound that pussy… it's yours- oh- oh God, yes, yes!

The orgasm came out of nowhere, rushing over her, leaving her a limp, shaking mess. He fucked her through it, drawing out her pleasure and driving her down into the desk so that her heavy breasts and stiff aching peaks dragged across the wood through her silky blouse. His body bore down on her, pinning her there so all she could do was struggle against the silk binding her wrists in a desperate need to grab something. the desk, him, anything that might give her a little leverage.

She shouldn't have liked it, but she did.

She never would have thought she could enjoy sex restrained, but this feeling of being under his control, powerless, at his mercy.

It was dark, primitive and so wild.

He knew just how to treat her.

He was splitting her open. Using her like a bitch in heat, and it was such a turn on.

She couldn't bear it. She needed to grab something, anything…

"Yeah, that's it, cum for me, you bad girl, cum all over my cock… mmm… spread that ass for me, show me your pretty little hole," Richard growled, drinking in the sight of Scarlet's bound hands grabbing her smooth alabaster cheeks, those perfectly manicured nails biting into the soft skin, spreading them wide to show him the tight rosebud nestled within.

The vision sent a hot shiver of lust down his spine, and he couldn't resist brushing it with his thumb, circling the sphincter, pushing in ever so slightly.

Scarlet could only gasp at the feeling against her pucker, the sensation causing her sex to clench around him. "Yes Sir… please, punish me, I need it… I… I…"

"As you wish."

He growled and Scarlet could have screamed as he pulled out.

Then his arms were around her and she came up and away from the desk. Then, as if she were as light as a feather, he hoisted her to her feet and walked her around the desk to the window.

"Put your hands on the glass," Richard instructed, the tie coming undone with a quick tug.

"What?" she asked, looking out the window, down across the canal, and the bustling hive of activity that was Gloucester Docks, where the whole of the city seemed to be wandering amongst bright colourful stalls.

He couldn't be serious. All it would take was just one person looking up and-

"Do it," he urged, slapping her ass again, the crack as sharp as a bullwhip and the sting enough to overwhelm caution.

She did as he commanded, bending forward slightly and pressing both hands against the window, the glass misting with her breath. "Good, now stay right where you are."

"What!" she snapped, her heart pounding in her breast. "Are you mad? The market's down there… someone might see, *Sir*."

"And I bet that gets you wet," he retorted, crouching down and nudging her thighs further apart so the musky scent of her sex fogged his thoughts. "Mmm… your cunt's all pink and slick and begging me to keep fucking her."

"No, Dick, please, that's… not fair. I don't- oh!"

He pushed a finger along her swollen folds, through her slick cream and into her lush depths, all the way to the knuckle. "Your dripping, you bad girl. Say it."

"No, please…" she panted, biting her lip to keep from moaning at the tingling shooting through her core. However, there was no resisting the choked sob as the digit twisted and curled, feeling and rubbing all of her most sensitive places at once. Nor could Scarlet stop herself from pushing back against him, her sex clenching. "Mmm… No! Wait, not here, there are so many people down there, what if someone looks up, they could see- "

"So what?" Removing his finger, he reached out and took her last few strawberries from the desk, crushing them to a juicy pulp in his hand. "Let them look, go on, let them see you for the little slut you are. Let the *whole damn city* see you for who you really are," he said, before putting his hand on her inner thigh.

"Stop… You can't… I'll scream…" Scarlet gasped, shaking as her clit pulsed at the feeling of his hand and the illicitness of the strawberry juice sliding over her skin, spreading it up her leg and over her butt. Then, it wasn't just his hands.

"Go ahead, scream all you want, that'll just make everyone look, won't it?" Richard said, following the sticky trail with his tongue, greedily licking up both the sweetness of the fruit and the salty flavour of her desire. "Maybe even someone in the office will hear and come running. Wouldn't that be something? Is that what you want, Scarlet? To prove all those dirty gossips, right?"

"No," Scarlet choked out, shaking, the throbbing of her core growing ever stronger as the slick glide of his tongue swept up her inner thigh.

"Then shut the fuck up before I gag that pretty mouth of yours," Richard barked, before pivoting and covering her swollen clit with the lush heat of his mouth.

Scarlet couldn't stand it.

His words were so dirty and crude, raw with lust. No one had ever spoken to like that.

It was such a fucking turn on.

She couldn't bear it. Just keeping her hands on the glass was torture in itself. She wanted to grab him, fist his hair, sit on his face, squeeze her tits, rub her clit, something, anything to-

"Oh… Oh my God… oh fuck-yes!" She gasped and moaned, squeezing her eyes shut against the feeling of sensory overload as he sucked hard and greedily on her little bud before lashing it with his tongue.

"You want to get caught, don't you? Yeah, I know you do. Your pussy's so juicy. Just the thought of it has your greedy little cunt all soaked. Don't pretend you don't like it. You're dripping for it…"

"No… *Dick*!… that's not- don't say things like that! Mmm… I can't help it… you're making me… oh no, no, please, if you do that… I'll…"

She was shaking, the waves of sensation crashing over her so violently her legs were in danger of giving way from under her as her fingers clawed the window for something, anything, to hold on to.

However, Richard showed no mercy.

"You'll what? Go on Scarlet, tell me," he pressed, swirling his tongue around the bundle of nerves, his hands fastening to her quivering hips, dragging them closer…

"I'll- oh fuck… oh my God… I'll… I'll…" She was mindless with the raw need to cum. And so close, when

his tongue suddenly abandoned her clit to drag along her folds, the world shattered around her. "Oh God, yes, yes, fuck yes, I'm cumming, I'm cumming, I'm cumming, fuck, fuck..."

Richard tongued her through the climax, not stopping even as her hips trembled in his arms. For what he had in mind, he wanted her good and relaxed. "Yeah, that's it, go on Scarlet, cum for me, let the whole damn city see you cum!"

She bowed her head to press her forehead against the window as the waves crashed over her, the glass deliciously cold against her flushed skin. "No... please... why are you doing this to me, please, I can't take it- oh fuck, yes, yes!"

"Mmm... beg all you want, Scarlet, this is the mouth that doesn't lie." Deaf to her pleas, he buried his face in her cleft, devouring her with long deep licks, his tongue swirling while the rough of his jaw scrapped oh so deliciously along her inner thighs. "You love it. Say it."

Scarlet shook her head, but the words stuck in her throat. She was shaking, powerless against the urge to grind back onto his tongue as her clit pulsed and throbbed, pleading for just that little bit of attention to send her soaring to the starry heavens. "No! Please don't make me- oh fuck, oh fuck, okay, okay, yes, I love it, I love it! Use me, abuse me... please, please, please, I'm your naughty little fuck toy... oh God... that's your pussy, that's your pussy..."

His cock jumped at her wanton tone, but Richard pushed on regardless.

Not yet. She wasn't ready yet. Just a little more...

"So now you don't want me to stop?" he asked with a mock teasing tone, pulling back just enough to drag the flat of his tongue along her folds, from clit to base, then back again in longer and longer glides.

A shudder wracked Scarlet at the suggestion. Or perhaps it was another orgasm. "No, no, don't stop, don't stop, please, put your dick back in me, fuck me against the glass for the whole world to see, make me cum all over your big hard cock."

"No," he rasped, his tone low and primal as he worked his tongue higher, hands spreading her cheeks. "I'm not done with you yet."

"What-oh!" Scarlet gasped as warmth washed over her pucker, sending shivers racing up her spine and throwing fresh fuel on the already raging lusts. Then his tongue slid up to circle her virgin hole, teasing it with gently prods and flicks.

No one had ever done anything like this to her before. It felt strange, dirty and wrong, but so exciting. "Wait! No... no, not there, please- oh fuck!"

She panted, her back curling at the feeling of his tongue pushing through her tight ring of muscle. Then her mind went blank, consumed by the sensation of wet heat sliding in and out.

"Wow Scarlet, I've barely started rimming you and you're already drenching the floor. Who would have ever guessed you were such an anal whore, and in front of the whole city, you bad girl." He swatted her arse just hard enough for the pain to heighten the pleasure. "Just look at you, you're loving this, aren't you?"

"Yes! Yes, I'm a bad girl, your bad little slut, punish my little hole, I deserve to be punished… I deserve it… I… I-"

"Have the tastiest ass," Richard growled, leaning over her, his body caging her against the glass as powerful fingers fisted in her hair and dragged her head round. Then he took her mouth in a bruising kiss, his sinful tongue encircling hers, brushing and stroking and fogging her thoughts with his strong, heady flavour.

No, not his flavour, hers. He was forcing her to taste herself.

The revelation made her core clench at the very moment he slid inside her.

"Mmm… I could fuck your cunt all day, you bad girl," Richard groaned, his dick painfully hard and the temptation to give himself over to the feeling of her lush walls milking him was almost irresistible. Almost. Instead, he rolled his hips, stirring her grasping sheath before pulling out, his shaft slick and glistening with her cream.

Scarlet shuddered at the loss and made a pouting sound that dissolved into a low moan as he leant down to nibble the shell of her ear, hands dropping to her naked ass, spreading her cheeks for his cock to glide up, the broad crest parting her folds.

She was shaking, so on edge, her whole body was almost humming with carnal need. One little push would be all it took to push her over the edge-

"But now…" he whispered in her ear, pausing only to bite down and tug on her lobe. "I want to find out how tight your ass really is."

She stilled at the dark promise in his voice, eyes widening as the crown touched her pucker.

"Wait, you don't mean? Oh no…" she gasped, shaking her head.

"Oh yes, your ass is mine," he growled, rearing back to drink in the vision of her stretched out before him. Flushed and panting, her blonde hair had become a passionate mess and that once immaculate white business dress was rumpled the way that only a good, hard fucking could do, its skirt scrunched up around her hips to show off the full curves of her luscious, strawberry smeared butt.

It was a complete contrast from the woman he knew and filled him with a savage, primitive pride. He slid forward, pressing his slick tip against the ring of muscle. Soft and pliant from the multiple orgasms, her body opened before him.

"Oh fuck! Oh, fuck!" Scarlet gasped, her eyes going wide at the sudden burning sensation, the feeling of something hard, thick, and slick splitting her open. Instinctively, she tried to clench down, to force him back, but that only seemed to speed his invasion on, so the broad crest slid through.

"That's it Scarlet, let me in… mmm you really are a tight arsed bitch all right, but don't worry, not for much longer," Richard promised, curling his hips in small circles, trying to resist the feeling of her body wrapping around his crown, sucking him in. He needed to loosen her up first, or else this would hurt.

Scarlet could only groan. Somewhere, deep down and far away, a little voice was screaming for her to give herself over to him, to let it come, but she couldn't. She just… couldn't. He was too big. Too thick.

She'd never felt this full, so stretched. So...

She threw a look back over her shoulder at him, her blue eyes large and pleading. "S-sir, I..."

Their eyes met and she couldn't keep her gasp at bay at the wild look burning in his eyes, the warring emotions battling just beneath the surface. It was the most savage look she'd ever seen, the reflection of the beast that lurked in the heart of every man as he was visibly torn between restraint, and the instinctive desire to fuck, to rut and claim her as his bitch.

His grip on her tightened, the fingers biting into her hips, holding her still as he took a step forward, pressing her to the glass while his dick kept working back and forth, slick with their mixed juices, sending heat rushing through her.

"No, Scarlet, look straight ahead."

She obeyed, too far gone now to turn back.

Overhead, the sky had turned a deep lilac, slashed with shades of pink and orange that danced across the waters of the canal as the sun slipped away behind the horizon. Below, the fair was still in full swing and growing busier as people finished their work and came to browse amongst the stalls. Anyone could look up and see them.

Someone already was.

Her reflection stared back at her from the window, but with the face of a stranger, with flushed skin and a hooded gaze, framed by a dishevelled mess of spun gold.

Bent at the waist, she looked shameless, like a whore just begging to be fucked.

The sight was so erotic, she couldn't bear it and tried squeezing her eyes shut against the image, but it lingered, burned into her mind.

"No, watch Scarlet, I want you to see," Richard bit out, his voice low and so dark with lust that she couldn't resist. Her eyes locked to his in the glass, and his hips snapped forward, driving his cock into her heat.

"Oh!" she gasped, fighting the urge to close her eyes against the sudden rush of hot sensations. "Oh fuck… oh fuck… You're… you're in my ass… there's a dick in my… oh God, this feels so…." She could feel herself opening to take him all the way, her forbidden little hole stretching to fit him, and only him.

Richard pulled back slowly, letting half of his length slide out, then drove back in, drawing another ragged sound from Scarlet. It was a deliciously snug fit, with her inner walls wrapping around him like a fist in a warm velvet glove, squeezing him tight, trying to milk the cum right out of him with every stroke.

"Yeah… you like it, don't you?" His voice was thick and gruff, more beast than man. With each push and slide, his hands dragged her into the saddle of his hips, inch by hard throbbing inch until he was balls deep.

"Yes!" she gasped, surrendering to the sinfully wicked sensations rippling out from her ass, making her clit throb and nipples ache. "Oh my fucking God… this feeling, it's so… so intense, I- I love it…. don't stop, don't stop…"

"Don't worry, you bad girl, I won't stop..." he promised, his eyes drifting down to watch his dick sliding in and out of her forbidden little hole. "Yeah, that's it, mmm… goddamn, you're taking it up the ass like a proper little whore now."

"Oh God, yes… yes Sir, I'm your whore, please, fuck me, harder, make me feel every inch of that big cock pounding my tight little virgin ass." Not caring if they were discovered, she pushed against the window to meet each thrust, grinding herself back onto his cock.

"And whose ass is this, my little whore?"

The words came unbidden.

"It's yours, all yours. I'm your good little anal whore. Split me open on your dick, make me take it. I love your cock in all my holes!"

"All of them? Even this tight little virgin ass?" he grunted, the slap of flesh meeting flesh rising around them, his movements growing more urgent with the feeling of his release building.

She bowed her head, pressing her brow to the window, the glass deliciously cool against her flushed skin. "Yes! All of them! I love taking it up the ass for you. I'm your naughty little office whore, that's just another hole for you, only you- oh fuck, oh fuck, Sir, please!"

"Please what?"

He was close, so fucking close. Not sure how much longer he could last, he pushed one hand down beneath the folds of her skirt, into the bounty of lush, wet heat. He was close, but so was she. He could feel it and rubbed her clit while fucking her with a single-minded need to make her cum just once more.

"Punish me. Sir, please punish me, I deserve it! Punish me, punish all of my holes every day." Scarlet couldn't breathe, couldn't think, she could only feel. Feel the heat and fullness moving through her ass, the waves crashing over her as rough fingers strummed her throbbing clit and turned her legs to jelly. "My ass is yours, all yours whenever you want… fuck, I'm gonna cum, oh fuck, oh fuck, I'm gonna cum on your cock, oh my fuckin… yes, yes, make me cum on your fucking cock! Fuck that ass, it's yours, all fucking yours, oh fuck, oh fuck, I'm cumming, I'm fucking cumming! I'm-oh!"

Her orgasm exploded through her, unlike any release that had come before, sending her soaring. Then she started to shake as the aftershocks claimed her, and Richard couldn't resist the feeling of her ripple around his thick, swollen cock.

"Yeah, that's it you naughty whore, cum for me, cum for me in front of the whole goddamn city- ah shit, I'm cumming too!"

He moaned, burying his cock in her one last time as he came, hard. Hard enough for small black spots to dance before his eyes.

Amidst the fog of her climax, Scarlet felt his release like a flood of heat deep inside her. It was the first time a man had ever come inside her, and she liked it.

He'd stained her, branded her with a mark that could never be erased.

It made her feel dirty, deliciously dirty.

She wanted more.

Chapter Seven

For the longest moment, Richard just watched Scarlet, the beast in him wanting to savour its victory, burning the sight of her stretched out beneath him into his memory.

Then the moment passed, and it plunged him face first into cold reality.

Oh fuck…

Scarlet looked back at him over her shoulder, her full lips half curling with that damn mocking smirk. "Mmm… was I a good little whore for you, Dick?"

"Knock it off, this… this was a mistake." He stepped back and quickly shoved himself into his trousers.

She cooed and wiggled her ass, her rosebud agape and weeping pearl tears. "*Aww*… what's the matter

Dick, the bitch going to throw a fit if you're late?" Her eyes flashed, daring him to bite.

"Fuck you," he snapped, resisting the sudden urge to put her over his knee, his nose wrinkling as his fingers fumbled with his belt buckle.

She straightened up and turned to face him, but made no effort to straighten the skirt still hitched about her hips. "We already played that game, remember?"

She lightly teased the petals of her sex with a finger before bringing the shiny digit to her lips.

"Yeah, well, maybe I'd rather forget." He wheeled around and walked around the desk, refusing to watch, and doing his best to ignore the still obvious stiffness straining against his trouser leg.

No, he wouldn't be tempted again.

However, Scarlet would not be dismissed so easily. Coming up behind him from the desk's other side, she slid her hands around his waist to finger his shirt buttons while rising up on her tiptoes to nip his ear. "Aww… don't be like that, lover. Come on, why don't you let me take care of that for you? You don't really want to go back to Alice smelling like sex, do you? There's a private washroom and shower in Daddy's office. I could wash your back for you and-"

"Forget it Scarlet!" Richard snapped. Angry and tired of her games, he brushed her hands away and rounded on her, so they were almost nose to nose. "This never happened, got it."

Scarlet held her ground, however, her playfulness gone, melted away to reveal an expression as cool and hard as ice. All except her eyes. They burned hot and fierce. "Don't kid yourself, Dick, that was the fuck of the century, and you know it. How long has it been since Alice fucked you like that? You think your little shop girl can?" Her smile spread wide, as cruel and sharp as a knife. "You're going to want it again."

She was right. About everything.

He wanted her. How could he not? He was only a man of flesh and blood, while she was the boss's daughter.

A young woman with a future as bright as her past was murky, a beautiful girl who played men the way a croupier dealt cards.

She was intelligent, sexy, and a damn great fuck.

She was Scarlet Holmes, his rock bottom, and he'd hit it hard, in more ways than one.

Now it was time to pick himself back up again.

So he turned his back on her and walked to the office door. Pulling it open, he didn't bother to look back. "Goodnight Scarlet."

At his back, still where she had stood, he could practically hear Scarlet seething when she hissed at his back. "I always get what I want, *Dick*."

It was the first time he had ever heard her composure crack.

He knew he should keep walking, to just let it slide, but sometimes he just couldn't help himself. "Then why don't you go up to your dad's office and fuck him instead?"

"Suck my clit you son of a- "

He pulled the door shut on her rebuff, and something smacked against the door. Something heavy.

Well, there goes my lateral move...

When he arrived home, the flat was dark and quiet.

It was only a short walk from the Docks, but he'd taken a detour to the 24-hour gym in the Gloucester Quay's, for a quick shower. Free membership was one perk of working for Holmes & Raine, and Scarlet had been right. He certainly didn't want to go home reeking of sex.

Freshly washed but still none the wiser as to what he was about to say or do, he'd practically dragged his feet all the way home. By the time he arrived at the tower block, the sun had long since gone down. Alice's car was in its usual parking spot, but a quick glance at the dark living room confirmed there was no sign of her inside. Nor Alexander.

He checked his phone to see if she'd tried to message him, but the screen stayed blank. The battery had died.

"Shit," he cursed quietly, the discovery winding his guts into a tighter string of knots. He'd been so out of it recently; he couldn't even remember when he'd last charged the phone. God only knew when the thing had died on him.

Had something happened to her? What if she or little Alex had had to be rushed to hospital? What if...

What if something hadn't happened...

What if she'd got worried because he was so late and tried to call him? What if, when he hadn't answered, she'd decided to check on him?

Just the prospect sent a cold shiver down his spine.

Had she seen them in the window? He'd been half expecting to get his collar felt the moment he'd left the building. Anyone could have seen and reported them to the police. Or perhaps he just missed her when he left the building and she'd run into Scarlet.

He had to know. He needed to speak to her. Maybe there was still time to – *what the fuck!*

He flipped on the living room light, about to plug the phone into the charging outlet there, when he heard it. A moan. Low and husky and *very* familiar.

Then the sound of wood creaking.

Bed springs squeaking

Someone calling.

Calling her name.

Then he was running through the room and down the hall to *their* bedroom door. A hard kick sent it swinging inward, and he stopped dead, his eyes widening at the sight of the bodies tangled together on the bed.

Alice… and Rebecca!

Sweet Temptations:
MÉNAGE À TROIS

THE LORD OF LUST

L.M. MOUNTFORD

Sweet Temptations:

MÉNAGE À TROIS

L.M. MOUNTFORD

Chapter One

Alice Martin wasn't a woman to beat about the bush.

She knew what she wanted and when she saw it, she went for it.

It had been that way the night she first met her husband. It hadn't mattered that he was at work or that they hadn't formally met, or didn't even know each other's names. She'd seen him, she'd wanted him, so she took him.

If she wanted something, the technicalities just didn't matter.

So when she saw a particular garment hanging in the window of the Bristol high street's *Sweet Temptations* Boutique, and felt that all too familiar draw, it had only been a matter of time.

Now fresh from a shower, with her hair still damp and her latest purchase hanging from her shoulders, she couldn't help grinning as she admired her reflection in her vanity.

The cherry red spaghetti strap gown was pure mulberry silk with a black lace trim and clung to her body in all the right ways to emphasise her curves and mile-long legs.

It was perfect. Richard wouldn't know what hit him.

Just the thought of modelling it for him when he came home, of lying stretched out across their bed waiting for him to find her and fuck her brains out, sent a delicious thrill sizzling through her. Beneath the silk, her poor neglected pussy clenched, and her clit, still stiff and begging to be played with, throbbed, reminding her of how close she'd come during that session she'd orchestrated for him during her break.

Damn her and her blasted ideas. This wasn't how it was supposed to be. That call was only supposed to be a warmup *for him*. A tease to get *him* worked up and hard and oh so desperate to take her. Instead, it had backfired and left her feeling restless and on edge. She'd been unable to settle her mind on anything. In short, she was so fucking horny, it was all she could do not to fish out 'Antonio' from her bedside draw and start the party early.

Just the thought of the wand's intense vibrations rumbling against her pussy had her thighs rubbing together in a vain effort to settle the need burning inside her.

It would have felt so good too, but instead she forced herself into action and, taking the matching robe from the hook on the door, she turned and hurried out into the hall. There was too much left to do. She couldn't afford to indulge herself, yet.

Especially when, so far anyway, everything had been going according to plan.

Everything was arranged. She'd left work early to beat Richard home, dropping her last class of the day on a colleague who owed her a favour and missing the ever notorious M5 rush hour. Her parents had said they were fine looking after Alexander for a couple of nights so he was all taken care of, and she had sent everyone else they knew a polite, but firm, text message, warning they weren't to be disturbed.

Tonight was to be theirs.

A quiet candlelit evening just for them, to let go of all their woes, reacquaint themselves with each other's bodies, and give in to all their carnal desires.

It was just what they needed. What they both needed.

Though he said nothing about it, she knew Richard had been feeling stressed. It was all the usual stuff, really, just the little things. Under pressure at his new job. Worried about money. The stresses of moving to a new city and starting a family. Fairly mundane, but her husband had always insisted on dealing with it all by himself, and it was taking a toll on him.

She wanted to help ease his burden, to take them back to how they used to be, even if it was only for one brief night.

And there was always that other thing.

That one little thing a small part of her was so insecure about.

Alice wasn't usually the jealous type, but where Richard was concerned, she was possessive. She was possessive as hell, and it had not escaped her notice that other women were taking an interest in her husband. Of course, he had always been a good-looking man, but age, it seemed, agreed with him. The cute puppy she'd cornered in the stockroom had grown up into a fox that any red-blooded woman would have to be blind not to notice. And when they did, she had to resist the urge to go up to them and claw their eyes out.

Normally, she had the urge under control. However, Scarlet's undisguised flirtations at the party had been the last straw.

Richard was hers. Her lover. The father of her baby. Her soul mate, and it was time she reaffirmed their bond.

Just imagining all the ways she could have her way with him, could brand him, mark him as hers, had her lip twisting devilishly as she slipped into the kitchen to rummage through the fridge. She could get the ice cream out now, so that it melted a bit first. Or maybe it would be better to start with the wet celery, as they still had the flying helmet from that Halloween party the year before they moved and she could always use the egg whisk on his-

A frantic shriek sounded from somewhere on the floor above.

Chapter Two

What the?

Alice's eyes widen at the sound, so high with pain and fear, like an animal caught in a trap. Forgetting her train of thought, her eyes darted up to the ceiling. It sounded like it had come from the Blaire's flat, but that could have been a trick of the building. The tower block's walls were paper thin and often as not, she could hear several things going on at once from any number of directions that sounded like they were coming from somewhere else. Just the other night she'd been treated to overhearing one couple's marathon sex session that had clearly sounded like it was coming from that very flat upstairs, but couldn't. After all, Richard had been up there, helping Rebecca with her computer.

A pity, if he hadn't been upstairs, it would have made quite the mood starter…

Another scream went out, louder this time and much more distinctive.

Rebecca. Alice's heart leapt into her throat.

"You worthless bitch!" a gruff voice half slurred, half barked, followed by the crash of something heavy smashing into glass, shattering it. "Stay still!"

Alice didn't wait for him to get his eye in.

Wheeling on her heel, she made straight for her front door, hurriedly tying the sash of her robe as she went. Another scream, louder, echoing as footsteps ran down the building's stairwell. Then suddenly they were on the landing, running, growing louder by the second as Alice ran to the door.

No sooner had she wrenched it open than Rebecca barrelled into her.

Just managing to catch herself, Alice pulled the girl to her, her arms going around her in a protective hug. "Hey, hey Rebecca, honey, what's happened? What's going on?"

"He's coming, please... I didn't touch... don't let him..." Sobbing, she clung to the older woman, her big doe eyes pleading, so wide they were almost round. The poor thing was terrified out of her mind.

The sight tore at Alice's heart and she pulled her closer, doing her best to sooth her with quiet words. "Shh... honey, it's okay, I won't, nothing's going to happen to you, I promise."

She almost couldn't believe this was the same girl she knew. Rebecca was always so upbeat and bubbly. Of course, she'd known there were some problems in the home. Even a blind man could have seen was nervous around her father and that he could be hard on her, too hard sometimes, but this...

The thought lit a fire in her mother's heart that threatened to burn them both to cinders. That the brute could do this to his own daughter. Drive such a sweet girl to such a fit of terror, sickened her to her very core. What parent, no, what kind of fucking beast could do such a thing?

Struggling to keep her tone soothing, Alice slowly steered Rebecca inside. "Come on, let's get you inside and I'll-"

"Come back here you little bitch!" the other voice bellowed from above amidst a thunder of footsteps. Then he was there on the bend on the stairs, Derik Blaire, red faced with murder and madness scorching his wild eyes. "Where is it, I want it, you fucking whore," he seethed, half lumbering down the last few steps like a hippopotamus, not even seeming to notice Alice. "You hear me? You're a whore. Just a fucking whore, like that bitch mother of yours, now give it to me!"

Rebecca stiffened at her father's call, her knuckles going white like bone as she clung on with a death grip. However Alice hardly noticed as she turned to look at the man. With a gaze as cool as ice, she gently pried herself free. Then, with a gently push, she urged the girl inside the flat. "Go inside," she instructed, her tone firm but just soft enough so that Derik wouldn't overhear. "Lock the door. I'll knock and call for you when it's safe to come out."

"No, please... don't leave me, don't let him-" Rebecca's eyes were glassy with tears and visibly pleaded for Alice not to leave her as she tried to cling to her arm. It was the same look she saw in the eyes of many kids on their first day of school, when their parents left them at the gates for the first time.

"I won't. Go on, I'll take care of this. You go put a brew on." It tore at Alice's heart, but she pushed her inside regardless and pulled the door shut with a firm slam.

She felt like a bitch for it but it was the only way. She couldn't deal with the problem at hand if she was concerned for the girl.

"What the fuck you think you're doing, bitch? Get the fuck out of my way!" he slurred angrily, staggering to a stop only a metre or so from Alice, swaying from one foot to the other. As if only just seeing her for the first time, he grinned in a way that made her feel dirty just for him looking at her.

"Alright *John*, I don't know what you're on tonight, but I think you need to go back upstairs and sleep it off." Alice wouldn't be cowed. He may have towered over her, but she was well accustomed to dealing with people bigger than her. She held his gaze with steely determination, doing her best to ignore the fact that the only thing protecting her modesty was a silk robe that showed off way too much leg and did nothing to hid the swell of her bosom.

"Don't you tell me what to do, you little cow," he slurred, sneering down at her. "I've had it with all you posh tossers… talking down to me… treating me like shit… That whore in there… took my shit… and now she's going to give it back or I'm gonna beat her ass black and blue then throw it out on the street." The thick stink of booze was coming off him in waves. He'd definitely had more than a skinful.

"No," Alice said firmly. "You're not going anywhere near her in that state. So just go back upstairs before I-"

"You'll what?" Derik Blaire barked, his mouth spreading into a mocking grin that could have curdled milk as he stepped forward, closing the gap. "What are you gonna do? Don't give me all that shit… Your man's not here to protect you. What you going to do to me, you little bitch? How are you going to stop me from taking whatever I want from your fat arse…" The threats were almost as ugly as he was. With that squat face crowned by a brush of chestnut-grey hair and a body like a barrel that had been sat on by something heavy one too many times, he gave the faint impression of being the love child of Bruce Willis and Ray Winstone. Only without the charisma, good looks, or height.

He was taller than her though. And that must have made him feel cocky because he loomed over her. Enough that she knew he'd be able to see straight down the valley of her cleavage soon enough. One of his hands slowly reached out to touch.

"You know, I'm sick and tired of you and limp dick treating me like I'm shit. Don't know why a cunt like you puts up with him. Look at those fat tits and ass… come on bitch, let me have a feel… mmm… too good for him… maybe it's time I show you how a real man treats his bitc-"

His words died with a sickening wet crunch.

Just before his fingers could touch the slope of her right breast, Alice rammed the heel of her palm up into his nose. Blood arced, and he wheeled away, howling in agony.

"Don't touch me," she growled. The very idea of this *thing* laying a hand on her provoked a fresh surge of fiery rage inside her. How fucking dare he, this… *beast* think he could touch her, even lay a single, filthy fucking finger on her.

Derik Blaire gave no sign of having heard her, however.

"Bitch… you broke my nose," he spat out, glaring at her with both hands clamped up to the ruin of his nose. Blood was oozing out from between his fingers.

"Yeah, I did," Alice shot back, and slowly she sunk down into the ready stance her instructors had ingrained into her, ready to spring to the attack. It felt awkward to assume the position again, but once upon a time, the position had been as natural to her as any. "Try to touch me again, and next time I'll break your hand and shove it so far down your throat, you'll be scratching your balls."

His eyes widened, perhaps surprised by her threat, then narrowed dangerously as hate and anger burned through whatever was left of his common sense.

"Scratch this." He lunged, cranking his fist back and swinging it up and around. It was a decent effort. If it landed, it might very well have taken her head off, but he was nowhere near fast enough. Pissed as a skunk as he was, the attack was pitifully obvious and Alice danced away, ducking down under his arm then sidestepping as his momentum carried him by. Whatever it lacked in subtlety, the robe made up for in freedom of movement, if nothing else.

Derik wheeled around after her, faster than anyone could have expected from a man so deep in his cups, bellowing his fury like a barbarian. His second swing was smaller, but the distance between them was so slight, she couldn't dodge him this time. Nor had she meant to. Instead, she closed the gap. Stepping in and driving her left forearm up into the hook of his arm, stopping it dead, as she folded her right arm and swung it up, clubbing his broken nose with her elbow.

The sudden explosion of pain obviously seared across the man's brain as his head jarred back and as his knees gave way. He went down hard, collapsing on his back to lie in a heap, conscious but dazed and soon to be in a lot of pain.

Alice turned away, walked back to her flat door, raised a hand to knock, and the door open. Rebecca stood behind it, her eyes wide but her look of terror now replaced by a mix of puzzlement and disbelief. Clearly, she had been watching everything through the peephole.

"How…" she started but seemed to think better of it halfway through and instead went with. "I mean, he was, and you're so- I mean a…"

"My dad was in the SAS," Alice said, like that should have explained it all, stepping inside and shutting the door on the sight of Derik Blaire lying there on the landing, broken and bruised, like some beached walrus. "When the boys at school started teasing me, he had the PT instructors give me some private coaching, then had me doing drills with the lads at *The Lines* over the weekends. They even let me run the selection march across the Brecon Beacons over summer holidays, and no boy ever pulled my pigtails again."

That wasn't strictly true. There had been a few who had tried to make fun of 'the little girl', but they hadn't been laughing for long. A throat punch could be one hell of a punch line, especially when delivered by a girl half your size.

The memory made Alice's mouth curl, then she took in the sight of Rebecca's pale and haggard face and it fell away. "Come on, honey, let's go get you cleaned up."

Chapter Three

Richard's phone was dead when Alice tried to call him, probably because he'd been called into a last-minute meeting. Probably that bitch, Scarlet, trying to get her revenge. If so, there was no telling how long it would go on for, so she just fired off a quick text, explaining what had happened, in the briefest possible terms.

There was no need to go into details, no point worrying him.

Once the tick appeared alongside the message on the screen, showing the text had been delivered, she put it down on the side. With no further use for the device, she picked up her freshly brewed mug of tea and headed to the bathroom.

She walked in without knocking.

Inside, the air was hot and humid. The windows were fogged and condensation rolled down the tiled walls in rivulets as Rebecca sat in a bath of hot water, hugging her knees to her chest. She didn't look up as Alice sat down on the side of the tub, but she had got a little colour back.

Alice offered her the mug. "Here you go, honey. Have a sip of this,".

Rebecca, however, just kept her head down and stared blankly into nothingness. Or perhaps she was just too fascinated by the last few soap suds floating across the water's surface to notice.

Alice carried on regardless.

"Not thirsty?" She set the cup down on the floor, then softly started stroking the girl's thick waves of dark chocolate hair. "That's okay. Take as long as you need. You're safe, I promise…"

She had such beautiful hair, so thick and silky smooth. She should stop wearing it in that silly side braid. It suited her down, in a beautiful unbound wash that would probably go all the way down to her butt. And what a butt it wa-

No, stop it! Alice chastised herself. There was a time and a place for such thoughts, and this sure as hell wasn't the time. Though she could have thought of worse places than a hot bath and with that in mind, she decided there were better ways to comfort the lass, as well as keep her hands busy.

Rebecca instinctively stiffened as the older woman pulled her into a hug, but Alice did not pull back. Instead, she tried to draw her against her even tighter, rocking softly from side to side, desperate to give the girl all the feelings of closeness and security she knew she needed.

She softened slightly after a moment, then completely as inside, the walls began to crumble.

When she finally spoke, her voice was a whisper. "Really?"

Alice's heart soared, yet she kept her voice even and neutral to not spook the girl. "Really what, honey?"

"Safe?" Her voice was a little stronger with that one syllable, the hope behind it almost tangible, but there was a tremble there too, as if she hung on a knife's edge, about to fall through the ice at any moment. "You said I'm safe… did you mean it? Really?"

The desperate hope in that one question raked Alice and she could feel the tears burning at the corners of her eyes. God, what had that monster done to her? "Yes, of course I did, honey," she promised, "I promise. You'll always be safe with us."

The words sounded hollow to her own ears and woefully inadequate, but Rebecca must have heard the sincerity in them because, slowly, she tilted her head up. Her big doe eyes glistening as they met the older woman's. "Thank you."

It was all she could muster before the last of her walls came down. Her tears flowed freely as she threw her arms around the older woman and buried her head into the crook of Alice's neck, shaking with the sobs. Alice hugged her through it, doing her best to comfort her even as her face grew wet with her own silent sobs for the girl's plight.

"It's okay, I promise, it's all going to be alright," she soothed, lying as much as hoping, not really knowing what else to say. How could anything ever be alright again? Domestic abuse was an ugly thing, destroying even more lives than it took, and the effects could haunt the victims for years after. How was she ever going to live a 'normal' life?

Alice didn't have any answers, so she did her best to just comfort the girl as all her grief and fear came pouring out of her. Then, as quickly as it had hit, the storm passed.

"I'm sorry, oh god, acting like that, I'm so embarrassed…" Rebecca said when the tears ceased, her reddening eyes downcast and uncertain as she pulled away and slid back into the bathwater. Full as it was, the soapy water came up to the tops of her breasts.

"Honey, it's okay," Alice said gently, retrieving the mug from the floor and handing it to her. "Do you want to talk about it?"

Rebecca didn't respond. The question hung in the air between them. Alice waited patently. She didn't want to push Rebecca too far, but she also wanted to give her the chance to speak before the memories took root inside her, like a rot.

Slowly, Rebecca took a long swig of the tea, stealing herself. It would have been half cold, but it was better than nothing.

"*He* thought I'd stolen something." Rebecca spoke softly, but the venom with which she spat the word emphasised it more than if she had screamed it out. "Turns out he'd known all along I was saving up to move out. So, when he couldn't find something on his desk, he realised I'd had someone round…" Alice felt a lump forming in her throat, remembering how she had half encouraged Richard to go help the girl. "I told him I didn't know anything about it, but he didn't believe me, just started shouting things. He'd already had a lot to drink by the time I got home. Normally he stops after he's screamed himself out a bit, but this time he just kept getting worse, then when he started throwing things, I just panicked and ran."

"Oh, honey…" There were so many other things Alice wanted to say, to tell her, to reassure her things could get better, but when Rebecca began sobbing again, they all caught in her throat. Instead, she just pulled her back into another close hug.

Rebecca carried on regardless, the words pouring out of her in the rush of fresh emotion. "He never used to be like this. When I was little, he was always so kind and would play with me and take me out for drives or trips to the park, and then the pool or the cinema. But after mum left… oh god, what am I going to do now? I can't go back home, but all my stuff is up there, and I haven't got nearly enough saved to find a place of my own yet… so I… but how can I…"

Alice didn't have an answer. She didn't have any answers. How could she? The girl's world had just been turned upside down and inside out, then given her a prompt kick in the teeth for her trouble. It fucking sucked, but answers for things so large took time to be worked out. So, once again, she just held her, hugged her close, and let her get everything out. All the while enjoying the feeling of the girl's warm body pressed so close against her own through the robe.

She was sure Richard had thought she was joking, or just playing a game when she'd remarked on how beautiful the girl was. He wasn't completely wrong, but she wouldn't deny either that she had more than once admired the girl's long legs in those tight little jeans she always wore and wondered what it would feel like to have them wrapped around her head as she feasted on her sweet little pussy.

Such fantasies were her naughty little secret, and she'd never been ashamed of them, but she wasn't about to let them ruin her marriage either. It wasn't that she was in the closet, or that she'd ever officially claimed to be bisexual, but then, she'd never said she was straight, ether. Straight, Bi, Gay, they were all labels, and Alice hated labels. Why should she define herself, or for that matter, what made other people think they could brand her like a cow on the block?

She was just her. Alice Martin. Mother, wife and teacher, that was all and in that order. Everything else was no one else's business.

Then again, she'd never told him that when they'd first hooked up, she'd been involved in an unofficial, on again off again fling with her roommate Samantha. Nor that it had continued after they'd started going steady, and that it had only stopped when they'd got married. Even then, while they had both moved on and settled down into actual relationships, occasionally, whenever she or Sam had felt the itch, they would arrange a girl's night to relive old times.

Richard had never asked much about the nights, so she'd never lied to him about it.

It was foolish and reckless, she knew, and after, on the drive home, she always promised herself it would be the last. She loved her husband, but there was just something about sex with another woman that she craved as well. She just couldn't help it.

It was so thrilling, feeling the graceful softness of another woman's body on hers, the way they shuddered and writhed in the throes of ecstasy beneath her, and their sweet moans as they soared over the edge...

Not to mention their instinctive skill for knowing just how and when to touch. The old man's adage was very apt and true. Only a woman knew what women wanted…

"You can stay with us," she said without thinking. An idea spurred as much by the heat rising off the bath and the lush floral scent of the girl's hair fogging her thoughts, as the devious ideas haunting her fantasies. "Stay as long as you need."

It was a stupid idea, and Alice could have kicked herself for saying it. The flat was too small, there wasn't room for them all. Where would she stay? There were only two bedrooms, and only one bed… where would she sleep, in bed with her and Richard- *no no… don't go there, don't go there.*

But it was too late. Her mind was already swimming with thoughts and ideas…

Naughty, dirty thoughts and ideas that sent a tingle of delicious shivers straight down to her core, making her pussy slick and clit throb once more.

"What?" Rebecca gasped, stilling for a moment, her eyes going wide as she looked up slowly from Alice's shoulder. For the briefest moment, she looked terrified, yet no sooner had their gazes met than she looked down, her lower lip trembling. "Oh, um… thank you, Miss Martin… for everything, you've been so kind, and I… but I can't stay here, I don't deserve it… I… I…"

Her words came out in a rush, and the self-loathing in them set a fire in Alice's soul.

Raising a hand to Rebecca's chin, she tilted the girl's head so she couldn't look away. Her big doe eyes were round and questioning, desperate for comfort and reassurance. "Oh no, no, no… don't say that. You've done nothing wrong." Breathless, Alice could feel her heart racing as she slowly dipped her head down. "None of this is your fault."

Rebecca shook her head, to overcome by the moment to notice. "No, it's not him. I've done something… something horrible. I'm a terrible person and I don't deserve-"

Alice's mouth silenced any further objections.

Chapter Four

It was an accident. She hadn't meant to kiss her, but when the moment came, Alice just couldn't help herself. She crushed her mouth to Rebecca's soft pink lips, all the pent-up lust and desire that had been building up inside her, crashing over the banks and sweeping her away.

Perhaps shocked by the act, Rebecca didn't respond or pull away. Just made an adorable whimper in the back of her throat as Alice's lips slid over hers. Acutely aware of the gorgeous body against hers, so firm and tight but also soft in all the right places, Alice pressed on. Sliding her arms around her waist, she crushed her to her, making Rebecca gasp before thrusting her tongue into her mouth to feast on the sweetness within.

Deep down, a small voice warned that she should slow down. That she might scare the girl off if she was too forward too fast, but she couldn't help it. She wanted this little minx, wanted her in every way she could have her, and the fire raging down in her centre only drove her on. She kissed her hungrily, needing nothing else in that moment so much as to possess her, consume her, devour her completely. Her tongue curling round and round in the soft little brushes and slides that always made Alice's knees weak, until all the tension flowed from her young conquest in a low purring moan.

Then she was kissing her back, sucking on her tongue with a greedy hunger, those soft lips working up and down like she was sucking a cock. The very idea of it made Alice's skin tingle and pussy throb, and she couldn't help her own little moan when Rebecca grabbed her. One hand fisting her hair while the other clawed at her ass through the silk, almost dragging her into the tub. It was a deliciously aggressive act that she would never have guessed would explode from her doe-eyed babysitter, and one that pushed all her hot buttons. She knew what she wanted, and with girls she always enjoyed being the top, but it wasn't fun unless they played too...

Not to be outdone, however, she reciprocated, pulling the girl up and out of the bath. Water ran off her in a shower of rivulets and miniature waterfalls, splashing across the floor, but Alice hardly noticed or cared. She turned and backed her up against the bathroom wall, pushing one thigh between those long legs, pinning her there.

Rebecca gasped at the unexpected contact, her back curling in sweet surprise. Greedily swallowing the sounds, Alice slowly rocked and ground her thigh against the girl's bare pussy, delighting in the feeling of her slick heat. When she couldn't take it anymore,

Rebecca broke away, a long sultry moan pouring from the circle of her lips as the friction drove her wild.

"Mmm… I love the way you taste… so sweet and naughty… so sexy…" Alice purred, leaning up to tease Rebecca's ear with her tongue as Rebecca's hips continued circling against her thigh. Her pussy was drenched. "Mmmm… I can't wait to eat your pretty little pussy."

"Oh god… Mrs… Mrs Martin… wait… We shouldn't…" With her breathing ragged, the girl couldn't get the words out but rolled her head back, offering more skin.

"No, I want you." Dipping her head, Alice attacked the graceful slope of her throat with hot, fiery nips before soothing the tender flesh with her tongue. "I want you to cum for me. Right here. Right now."

"But what about… Mr Martin…" Rebecca got out, all the while trying to drag her ravisher closer. Her nails bit into her skin through her robe as she answered each grind with one of her own in a desperate plea for more. Her question fell off into another wanton moan when Alice sucked her pulse spot.

She wanted it. Alice knew it. She could see it written in her eyes, dark with lust. Had felt the truth of it in the heat and hunger of her kiss. Yes, she wanted this, but there was something else, something holding her back. Fear perhaps. Fear of the consequences, of what it could mean.

It didn't matter. By the time she was done, she'd have forgotten them all.

"I doubt he'd mind," she said, pressing her thigh a little harder against the girl's pussy and the little bundle of nerves hidden within. "Coming home to find his wife eating out their babysitter..." Her own heart was racing with the idea. Just picturing Richard walking in and finding them like this got her so hot, one of her hands came up to cup Rebecca's breast. It felt amazing. So soft but also full and firm and as incredible as she'd imagined, it filled her hand completely. The peaked nipple poked into her palm, begging for attention. "Do you think he'd join us right away, or sit back and watch?"

"Mrs... Martin... Please... I-I...." Alice's clit throbbed with each hitch in Rebecca's voice whenever she rolled her palm over the stiff peak. The sound was so delicious, she wanted nothing more than to fuck a few more out of her.

Reluctantly, Alice abandoned her prize to raise the hand up to Rebecca's check. Cupping her jaw, she gently angled her face so she was looking her in the eye, wanting her to see the truth in her words. "He doesn't know I like girls, too. Won't he be *surprised*. He might want to watch, but I think he'd rather join us. We talked about this just the other morning, after he helped you after you babysat for us."

"You did? But I thought you would be ma-" The girl's eyes widened and there was a tremor in her voice that had nothing to do with the leg pressing against her cleft. A hint of something Alice couldn't bear right now. So she silenced her with a kiss, sealing her mouth over Rebecca's and sliding her tongue in to chase the demons away with slow, luxurious licks.

"It got him so hard, thinking about your perfect tits and this cute little butt..." she growled huskily, sliding her other hand downward. Fingers outstretched and feeling their way along the smooth flesh, teasing along the swells of her buttocks to the lush heat beneath. "Oh, he became a beast, telling me all the things he would do to you… then I suggested sharing you…"

"Please… Mrs Martin… I… we- Oh!" Rebecca buried her face in the crook of the woman's neck, low moans flowing from her thick and sweet as honey. Almost of their own volition, her knees slid apart as the digits brushed along her slick folds.

"That's it, open up for me honey, yes, let me in, good girl… mmm… you're so wet." Sliding one finger through folds into the slick heat, she grinned inwardly at the feeling of Rebecca's walls clenched around her digit, begging for more. "He fucked me so hard and deep, telling me how good this sweet little pussy tasted… how much he loved the feel of it wrapped around his cock, milking out every drop of his cum…" The memory of his cock pummelling her poor pussy with a mad beastly intensity that left her aching and unable to walk straight for most of the day sent a hot shiver tingling through her.

"You… Oh god… You mean you don't… don't mind?" Rebecca's mouth pressed so close to Alice's ear she could feel her desperation shivering through her skin.

It gave her such a sense of conquest. Knowing she'd done this to her. Reduced her to this luscious little wanton. But it wasn't enough. She wanted to take her all the way. To take this little good girl to bed and draw out the sex kitten that lurked beneath the surface.

"Mmm… would you like that, honey? Is that what you want? To feel my husband go balls deep in this tight little pussy and give you the fucking of your life?" she asked, easing her finger out then back in, adding a second finger as she did.

"Oh!" the girl gasped, the feeling of crashing over her and carrying her away. "Yes… please… please… I… I… oh god, yes, please, I… I… want… it, I want it…"

"Mmmm… your so fucking wet." Alice didn't let up. Sliding her fingers in and out, she felt and teased every part of the slick, delicate tissues she could reach, trying to touch as much of Rebecca as possible. "Are you going to cum? You're going to get this pussy nice and creamy for my husband's cock. Yeah, that's it baby, say it…"

"Oh god, yes! Yes! Please Mrs Martin, I want it, I - oh fuck, oh fuck, fuck, fuck…" She was close. Growing more frantic, she arched up onto tiptoes and curled one long leg over Alice's. Granting her thrusting fingers deeper access as she circled her hips into each plunge.

Fuck, she was so sexy. Alice couldn't wait to have her spread out beneath her in her marital bed, watching her arch and scream and cum over and over as she did such wicked things to her. "Say you want it as I make you cum all over my fingers."

Curling her stroking fingers, she reached out to that spot of roughened flesh beneath her clit. One touch was enough to have Rebecca's back curling as she threw her head back with a shuddered moan of surrender. "Fuck, yes! Please, I want to fuck your husband again, Mrs Martin!"

"Good gir-" Alice froze, her sense of conquest suddenly forgotten as she realised what the girl had just said. "Wait, what?"

However, Rebecca didn't hear the question, or the dangerous lowness to her seducer's voice. Her every focus was on the fingers buried inside her, and the fact they had stopped. Breathing hard and ragged breaths, she shook her head, almost mad with her closeness, mindless with that desperate clawing need to cum. "No! No, please, don't stop, I want his cock again, Mrs Martin, please, please, let me fuck your husband again... please, please, plea-"

"What!"

Chapter Five

Her fury was cold and sharp, cutting through the spell of the moment like a knife.

"W-hat?" Rebecca blinked, confused, her voice shaky as she was rudely dragged back from the brink and thrown into icy reality by the sense of Alice's fingers leaving her.

Alice just glared at her, her eyes so cold they almost blazed. Yet, for all her palpable fury, when she spoke, her voice was even. "What do you mean 'fuck him again'?"

"You mean you didn't…" she began, shaking her head, as if not understanding the question. "But… but you said… he told you and you talked about-"

Alice rolled her eyes. "We role-played my over-hearing him fuck you that night, and-" As she said it, the wheels in her head suddenly turned and a piece fell into place. Realisation dawned, sending a cold wash cascading down her back to leave her legs feeling shaky. Her heart raced, beating a thunderous tempo in her ears. "Oh god, that was you! Wasn't it? Both of you." Her voice flared, going from icy cool to a raging inferno. "He fucked you that night, didn't he?"

Rebecca was shaking, her eyes wet and glassy. "Yes, but Mrs Martin, please I didn't, it just… happened, I never meant… I'm so sorry…" she sobbed, her words a desperate plea. But a plea for what? For her to understand? To forgive? Maybe both, or perhaps something else…

Alice searched the girl's face. Again, that small part of her spoke up. She wanted to believe her. There was no lie in her eyes. That was true. Only fear and worry. They were almost like the eyes of one of her pupils, when she'd caught them doing something they knew was wrong, and awaited the inevitable punishment. But just like those brats, there was no regret. She didn't regret having sex with her husband. In fact, she had probably been planning to do *him* again.

How fucking dare she!

She let out a sigh, jealousy enveloping her like the coils of a monstrous python. "No. No you're not. Not yet."

Rebecca's eyes went wide. She opened her mouth to say something, her pretty little mouth with lips swollen from the kiss, but all that came out was a squeak of surprise as Alice grabbed her arm. In no mood to hear whatever she had to say, she just spun on her heel and dragged her out the door, across the hall, and through the door to the master bedroom. Kicking the door shut behind them, she threw the girl to the bed, where she landed with a bounce. Then she just lay there, unmoving in a dishevelled, beautiful heap upon the bed, with her dark hair spread out beneath her, her eyes downcast, and puffy lips quivering.

The sight stoked the embers still smouldering in her core, and Alice slowly licked her lips, thirsty for another taste of the girl. She just looked so divine, like a feast spread out for her to devour.

"Mrs Martin…" Rebecca whispered, her voice shaky as Alice mounted the bed, planting both hands on either side of her shoulders, caging her with her body. "What're you-"

"Shut up," Alice commanded, the order firm despite the softness of her voice as she leant down, brushing the tip of her nose over the girl's. "Open that pretty little mouth without permission again, and I might just gag you up. Understand?"

Rebecca nodded, her eyes so big and wide as she bobbed her head up and down.

"Good, now stay right where you are…" Alice purred, dipping her head to slide her mouth over the girl's in a ghost of a kiss before sweeping her tongue across her soft pink lips. Immediately they parted in an instinctual plea for more as, despite the warning, she arched up to deepen the kiss.

Alice was faster, however. Greedy to taste more, she pivoted, dragging her tongue down the column of her throat before peppering hot, opened-mouthed kisses over the tops of her breasts. "Mmm… such beautiful tits…"

"Ah… Mrs Martin…" Rebecca panted, rolling her head from side to side as Alice's tongue circled her nipple in a tease at the things she had in store for her.

"You like that? Want more?" Alice purred, keeping her voice low so each syllable would tingle through the tender flesh.

God, it would have been so easy to go down on her right there. To throw caution to the wind and do everything she'd thought about doing to this little tease. To live out all her dirty, little, private fantasies. All it would have needed was just that one little push.

"Yes… yes… I want it… want more…" The words came out in a hot mess as Alice took the pebbled flesh between her lips and sucked. "But why… I mean… oh fuck… you don't seem very… or shouldn't you be more… mmm… mad at me?"

"Oh honey, I'm not mad. I'm furious," Alice promised, her eyes bright with a predatory gleam as she watched her twist and writhe under her sensuous assault. There was nothing sexier than watching a lover come undone. "How dare he keep you from me." She pulled away with a slow draw, lingering just long enough to graze her teeth along her assaulted nipple. Rebecca hissed with the light sting of pain, but Alice soothed it with a swirl of her tongue before switching to its twin. "Mmm… Just look at you. So sexy. You're perfect… my husband's perfect little toy." It was impossible to keep the edge from her voice at that. Just the idea gnawed at her like a dog with a bone, fuelling the blaze in her core. "Well, not anymore. You're my toy tonight."

"Yes… please… do whatever you want to me," Rebecca entreated, her voice rising in a sensuous moan as Alice worshipped that nipple the way she had the first. She couldn't help herself. The girl was just so sweet and lush, a feast spread out to be devoured.

Nothing, not even the dirtiest and kinkiest of all her wildest fantasies, could compare to reality. Eager to begin, she pressed a hand between Rebecca's thighs, cupping her mound and sliding two fingers into her drenched heat.

"Oh, your pussy's so wet for me, you dirty girl," Alice said, abandoning her breasts to take her mouth, swallowing the long moan that flowed as sweet as honey as she swirled her digits through her cream. Once they were liberally coated, she pulled back and raised them up so they could both see they were slick and shiny. "I'm going to make you my obedient little fuck toy, but first, I want to see if your pussy's as sweet as your perfect tits."

Eyes locked with Rebecca's, she gave her forefinger a slow seductive lick before putting it in her mouth and sucking it clean, moaning at the musky flavour. "Mmm… you're delicious," she purred, then offered the other finger to the girl. "Wanna taste?"

For a moment, she looked like she might try to refuse, but when Alice pressed the glistening tip of her finger to her lips, they opened obediently. Her tongue slid out to swirl around the digit, licking up the juices coating it before taking it into her mouth, sucking greedily.

"Yeah… that's it, suck it clean, taste your sweet little pussy," Alice ordered. The sight and sounds of the minx's mouth sucking her own slickness from her fingers getting her wetter by the second.

Had she sucked Richard's cock this way? Strangely, the thought didn't inflame her ire, but made the throbbing of her clit so intense, it took most of her willpower to resist the urge to rub it right there and then. So hot and greedy, she was probably a good little cock sucker.

When Rebecca released her finger, sucked clean, Alice smirked down at her. "So, did you like your first taste of pussy?"

With her body almost quivering with need, the girl nodded but looked away from the older woman's knowing gaze.

"Do you want more?" Alice pressed, bending down to trail her tongue down that long neck before pulling back to blow softly over her nipples, stiff and begging for more attention.

Rebecca nodded again, biting her lip as shame and lust tinted her face an adorable pink.

"I can't hear you," Teasing, she dropped her hand to the girl's trembling inner thigh, close enough to feel the heat radiating from her cunt, the skin deliciously smooth and soft. Slowly, she reached a finger out to circle her clit.

"Yes!" Rebecca gasped, so mad with the need for release, the words came spilling out in a hot rush. "More… please… fuck me, Mrs Martin!"

Alice was happy to oblige.

"Mmmm… good girl…" she praised, sliding down her body and laying hot, open-mouthed kisses down her midriff and navel as she went. "You're so sexy… so perfect… my perfect little fuck toy…" With that final claim, she buried her face between Rebecca's legs, dragging her tongue along her folds from the base up to the clit.

"Oh! Oh fuck… Mrs- Mrs Martin…." Rebecca gasped, her head rolling back and body curling up into Alice's mouth as she licked up and down with long, lazy strokes. The flat of her tongue spreading her folds while the tip dipped in to slide through her tender tissues.

All the while she watched, peering up at the girl from between the V-junction of her legs, delighted in the sight of her arching under her mouth, writhing, head thrashing and eyes squeezed tight against the pleasure while her breasts rose and fell with ragged breaths.

"Does that feel good?" she asked, sliding up to circle her clit.

"Yes! Oh god, feels so good!" the girl choked out, completely overwhelmed and white knuckling the tangled bedspread in an effort to grind her hips against her tormentor's tongue.

It was one of the sexiest sights Alice had ever seen.

"You like me licking your pretty little pussy?"

"Yes!" she gasped, shaking with her need.

"Good," Alice purred, giving the girl's clit a sensuous kiss. The musky scent of her flowing desire curled up her nose, as addictive and intoxicating as spiced wine.

"Now whose pussy is this?" To emphasise her question, she plunged her tongue between her folds, licking every part of the slick honeypot she could reach. Heady cream poured past her lips as her tongue probed, twisted, and flicked.

"Oh fuck! It's yours! That's your pussy, Mrs Martin!" Fuck, it sounded so hot when she called her name like that.

"That's right. My husband was only renting it when he fucked it, but you belong to me now," she growled, pushing the girl's legs back towards her chest, opening her completely. Then, curling her arms around her thighs, she dragged her cunt to her mouth.

"Yes… Yes… it belongs to you… oh fuck!" The moans left her in a rush as Alice focused all her attention on her clit.

"Yes, that's it, your such a good girl, such a good little fuck toy… Mmm… you're so wet and taste so good… does my good little fuck toy want me to make her cum?" she asked, shaking her head from side to side so her tongue wouldn't lose contact with the little bundle of nerves.

"Oh fuck! Yes!" she gasped, her tone rising higher and higher while the muscles of her thighs tensed in Alice's hands, her restraining hold just managing to keep her pinned beneath her mouth. "Please… please, Mrs Martin… lick me… fuck me… I want to cum… I want to cum for you…"

"Then do it, you dirty girl, cum for me… cum in my mouth like the dirty girl you are," she ordered, before taking her clit between her lips, her cheeks hollowing as she sucked, hard.

"Oh-oh my god…" Rebecca sobbed, her spine curling at the delicious suction as her hands grabbed for Alice's head, fisting her hair. "Oh fuck… there… right there…. Fuck! Yes! Yes! Ye…" Her words trailed away as her orgasm hit, crashing over her like a tsunami. It didn't matter. Alice took everything she had to give, sucking her through the rolling waves as her hips curled and undulated, fucking her mouth in all the ways that made her own neglected pussy throb.

Especially when combined with the sheer eroticism of watching this beautiful creature cum. Of knowing she'd been the one to reduce her to such a state of base pleasure.

When the storm finally passed, Rebecca tumbled back down to earth and collapsed into the sheets in a quaking mess with a heaving bosom, glazed eyes and flushed checks of a woman well fucked. With a last cleaning lick, Alice disentangled herself. Shrugging off the hand that had been tugging at her hair, she crawled up her body to press an opened mouth kiss to her lips to feed her the last of her own sweetness. Even in her haze, the girl drank it greedily, sucking at the slickness from her tongue with a soft purring moan.

"So, how was it?" she asked, a knowing smirk pulling at the side of her lips as she pulled away.

Rebecca exhaled, her breathing ragged as she tried to gather her wits. "Amazing, Mrs Martin…" She pushed a hand through her bangs, brushing back the tangled tumbles of her hair that had stuck to her misted brow. "Oh god… my clit's still pounding, I can't feel my pussy…"

"Aw? You poor thing. Well, guess that means I eat pussy better than my husband then." Alice teased, rearing back to sit on her haunches. Hey eyes sliding down, the vision of the girl spread out beneath her, spent and ravaged and so beautifully fuckable.

"Well… I don't know if I'd go quite that far." Her eyes glanced away, her blush deepening, if that was at all possible.

The mock challenge sent a thrill straight to Alice's core that made her drenched cunt pulse.

"Oh really, you little minx? I guess that's it then, isn't it? I was going to go easy on you, but now I have to remind you of your place." She undid the belt of her robe and gave a shrug so it pooled around her feet, leaving her just in the gown. It took all her restraint not to rip that over her head, too. The cool night air felt delicious against her overheated skin.

Rebecca's mouth fell open. "Wow… Mrs Martin, you're beautiful."

"Mmm… flattery won't save you now, honey." She teased, another spike of pleasure searing out from her clit at the hungry look in the girl's eyes. It was nothing short of burning desire. "And what about my tits?"

"Your tits?" The words were tentative but she couldn't help staring as Alice leant forward just enough to emphasise the tops of her breasts, shown off perfectly by the deep cut of the silk and lace.

"Yes. Do you like them too?" she asked silkily, lowering a hand to cradle the back of the girl's head, raising her up. "Do you want to taste them? Suck on them?"

Rebecca's tongue licked across her bottom lip. "Yes. They're amazing, but I don't-"

Her words were smothered to silence when Alice pressed her face into her breasts. For all her outward nervousness, Rebecca didn't hesitate and applied lip service to every bit of skin she could reach, peppering the tops of her breasts with fervent kisses.

"Mmm… good girl, that feels… So good… yeah, worship my tits," Alice panted. It was a delicious sensation. The feeling of the mouth on her skin merging with the desperate heat burning inside her and sending tongues of tingling fire flicking over her skin, driving her wild. Fisting the girl's silky hair, she pressed her face hard to her breast, dragging her where she wanted with one hand while pushing the gown's spaghetti straps down with the other, freeing her breasts.

Rebecca didn't miss a beat and dragged her tongue over the dusky nipple, making Alice gasp and arch. Her head fell back with a pleading whimper for more as the girl's hands came up to cup and squeeze her cleavage, sending waves of ecstasy down to her core. Meanwhile, Rebecca's tongue rolled around and around her nipple, winding her up tighter and tighter, before switching to curl and flick over the other.

"Oh fuck, that's it… mmm… yes, suck my tits, show me what a good little fuck toy you are!" Alice moaned in a shuddering breath, the sight of that pink tongue sweeping over her breast working her into a frenzy. Her breasts, though always sensitive, suddenly seemed to be intensely so. The feeling was divine yet woefully inadequate and made her feel ready to burst. Then soft lips closed over her right nipple in a hard suck, and something inside her snapped. Unable to wait anymore, she dragged Rebecca's mouth from her breast and pushed her back down on the bed. She landed with a cute little gasp that was quickly silenced when Alice climbed up her body and sat on her face.

Later, the despicable part of her brain that deals with second thoughts and regret will try to convince her that this was a bad idea. That Rebecca was a girl-sex virgin and she should have found a better way of coaxing her through going down on a woman than just shoving her cunt on her face.

But at that moment, Alice didn't care.

She was desperate, near mindless with the need to cum, and the first stroke of her lover's velvety tongue was like a burst of white hot firecrackers behind her eyes.

"Oh fuck, yeah, that's it, lick my pussy… Yes! Yes!" she moaned, throwing her hands out against the nearest wall to steady herself. Her back bowed with the sensations radiating from her core as Rebecca's tongue went to work, sliding through her folds with long lapping licks that turned her legs to jelly. Turned on as she was, she knew she wouldn't last long.

Rebecca was a quick learner. While her first lick had been a shallow test, nervous and unimaginative, they quickly turned long and smooth. Then her hands were around her hips, hands grabbing and squeezing her ass, drawing Alice's cunt to her mouth as her tongue plunged deep, drinking her in like she was parched and dying of thirst.

No doubt about it, the girl was a natural pussy eater.

"Oh god honey, you've no idea how long I've wanted to see you like this…" Alice moaned. Just seeing her beneath her, those wide eyes staring up at her from between her thighs as she ate her was stoking the fire in her belly, her nerves from her clit to her nipples were on fire, the heat radiating out to her fingers and toes. "Mmm… your pretty little face between my legs… licking my cunt like the dirty girl you are… such a dirty… dirty gi- oh fuck, oh fuck!"

Whether on purpose or by chance, Rebecca had found her clit, and the feeling of her lapping at the bundle of nerves drove Alice wild. It all felt so fucking good. The tight tingling of her nipples. The throbbing knot at her centre. All The things she was doing with her mouth, that made it feel like her lips and tongue were everywhere, licking, kissing and sucking her all at once. It all came together, and she was about to burst.

"Yes! Yes… Oh god… that's it… suck my clit… make me cum on your face- oh fuck, oh fuck, oh fuck, oh fuck!"

Doubling over, she clawed at the wall for whatever purchase she could find as her hips curled and rocked, grinding her sex into the girl's mouth, riding her face as her release exploded through her. Rolling curtains of an aurora blazed across her eyes as her orgasm crashed over her in great white-capped waves, washing her away from her body into a sea of bliss.

She wasn't sure how long she floated there, but when she finally opened her eyes, never having actually realised she'd shut them, Richard was standing over her.

Chapter Six

Taking in the sight that greeted him on the bed, *their* bed, Richard didn't know what to say.

It was a new experience for him.

Good or bad, he usually could always be relied upon to spit out some sort of asinine observation. Of course, it wasn't every day you walked in on your wife riding another woman's face to what could only be described as an earth-shattering orgasm.

Especially when it happened to just be their babysitter's face she was riding.

The same babysitter who'd been under his desk sucking his cock that very morning.

Ironic, considering they didn't even like sharing cutlery at dinner.

"Well, when you said you had a surprise for me, I wasn't expecting this." He forced himself to speak, the words catching in his throat, as thick and sticky as toffee as the sight of them tore at him. Tore and slashed with icy talons set aflame. The blaze scorched the surface to black blisters while the icy edge cut deeper than bone. It left him numb to the world but merged with the guilt of his own misdeeds to plague his conscience. "You've surpassed yourself this time."

His voice's flat tone and that detached look shimmering in his dark eyes quickly hit Alice in a cold cascade that twisted her stomach into knots of dread. She had never seen her husband look so... She couldn't put a name to it. It was neither anger nor sadness, but something in between. Something that seemed to hone the sharp lines and smooth planes of his broad, handsome face, somehow making him even more devastatingly attractive. Lost, no, forlorn, that was it. She had never seen him look as forlorn as he did just then.

It tore at her heart to see him so wounded, and it hung a weight of guilt and regret about her neck. Whatever her reasons had been, she'd never wanted to hurt him.

However much Rebecca's confession had stung her, the betrayal was only an idea, while he was seeing her with his own eyes. Just the idea of being in his shoes, of walking in without warning to find him going balls deep in the girl's tight little cunt, was enough to make her feel sick.

He was taking it in his stride though and, for all her wanting to comfort her husband and tell him how much she loved him, she saw his challenge. Saw it and accepted it, refusing to falter under his cool glare, but met it head on. Her eyes were hard and challenging even as she gave him her best sexy, faux-innocent pout. "Surprise, *Dick*," she purred sweetly, bending a hand down to stroke Rebecca's hair. "Someone let slip about how you helped her the other night, and well, I decided she needed a little lesson in manners."

And not to fuck with other people's husbands.

"Really?" If he hadn't just walked in on it, it would have been almost impossible to tell she'd just come down from a hard orgasm. Her voice was just as sensuously throaty as he'd ever heard it. His eyes glanced down to where the top of the girl's head was peeking out from between his wife's thighs. She'd stopped what she was doing when he'd spoken, and her doe eyes stared up at him, wide and unsure. "Funny sort of lesson."

"You know me," Alice shrugged, pushing the locks of her dark hair that had tumbled across her face back into place. It was an offhand remark, but he didn't miss the hidden meaning behind the words.

Oh yes, he knew her. Alice was a vixen. Beautiful, strong willed, determined. A woman who knew what she wanted. She also loved her games and could be a right ball breaker.

Hell hath no fury, as they say, and Alice was definitely not a woman to scorn.

"Umm… Mr Martin, I'm er…" Rebecca spoke up, her voice shaky.

"Oh, I think you can call him by his name now, dear. I'd say we're all well past the formality stage." Alice cut in, only half teasing as she touched a hand to her hair and, without breaking eye contact with her husband, directed the girl's mouth back to her pussy. "And I didn't give you permission to stop."

They were going to continue with him still there, standing over them. It was like she'd slapped his face.

"Well, would you like me to leave so you can finish your lesson?" Richard asked, trying desperately to keep his voice easy despite the storm of tension gathering around them.

If she sent him away now, then it would be over. Them. Their marriage. Their family. Everything.

Alice held his gaze for a moment, considering. Time seemed to hold its breath, then a current suddenly ran through her and her head fell back with a long moan. "Go? Oh no, no, no, you silly boy, I'm only... only just getting started. Now it's time for you to get your lesson." With her hips gyrating, curling and grinding into Rebecca's mouth as the girl resumed tonguing her clit. She pointed towards the chair that sat in the room's corner. "Go. Si-sit over there- oh fuck, Mmm... I want you to watch. Watch your little slut make me cum again."

And without a word, Richard did exactly that.

It was odd. A part of him knew he should be and indeed was fucking furious. Furious at Rebecca. At Alice. At them both for what they'd done and what they were doing. However, there was another part, a much larger part, the part that had been winding itself up in guilt-ridden knots, that felt almost... relieved. He'd fucked up, he'd cheated, but now so had she.

People liked to say two wrongs don't make a right... and in an ideal world, they wouldn't, but the world wasn't a perfect place. Morally corrupt or not, revenge felt good.

So if this was what his wife wanted to do, to make herself feel better about the situation, who was he to stand in her way?

And after his own misadventures that day, with both Scarlet and Rebecca, it was a much more merciful punishment than he deserved.

Alice could have cried for joy at that moment.

She'd been so afraid. So terrified he might walk out of the room, and her life with it. The relief she felt, watching him drop into the armchair, mingled with the feel of the slick tongue fluttering over her oversensitive clit, almost made her cum again. No matter what, she loved her husband, and always would. She wasn't ready to lose him, but that didn't mean she wouldn't punish him when he'd been so naughty.

And he'd been a very naughty boy.

"Oh fuck! Yeah… that's it, slut, just like… oh fuck, oh fuck!" she moaned, the words leaving her in a rush, her hips curling, fucking Rebecca's hot little mouth as that wicked tongue fucked her. The knowledge that Richard was watching her do this turned her on more than she would have imagined. The throbbing in her clit and the waves of pleasure rushing through felt so much more intense this time round. It all felt so good. So good, her eyes instinctively closed against the sensation, but when she opened them again, it was to see her husband watching her from the chair.

And as their eyes met, it took everything Richard had to stay where he was.

Punishment be damned. His wife was trying to kill him, he was sure of it.

His cock definitely agreed. Despite its vigorous workout with Scarlet, the sight of his wife riding Rebecca's face had roused the organ to new life. It strained against its confines, forming a bulge in his crotch that ached for attention. Called out to be touched. Practically begged to be unleashed and plunged balls deep into either of their sweet creamy cunts.

It was a call impossible to ignore, and he'd almost had the button of his trousers undone when Alice noticed.

"No, *Dick,* oh fuck! No, don't you dare…" she warned in a sweet song of pleasure as, all her lingering inhibitions gone, Rebecca ate her eagerly. The pink of the girl's tongue was just visible between her thighs, sliding through Alice's folds before she switched to sucking at her clit. "Oh! Oh my god… This… this is a punishment, remember. Keep your hands at your side, and just watch. Watch your little toy eating your wife? She's all mine now. You can't touch her till I say, is that clear? Just sit there and watch me cum all over this little slut's face."

Oh yes, they were both definitely trying to kill him.

"Fuck… your such a tease," he groaned, stunned and barely able to believe his eyes, or his restraint. His mouth watered as he watched and remembered the succulent taste of his wife's creamy pussy and longed to be the one between her thighs, feasting on her cunt.

This was Alice he was watching, after all. His wife. His reserved but not at all repressed, little firecracker of a wife, riding the face of their babysitter and obviously loving it. How had he never known she was into girls? Fuck, just the thought of it drove him wild. Now his cock was so hard, it was really starting to hurt. The solid weight of it pushed against his trousers, so insistent it might very well rip through the fabric.

"Oh no, Dick… this isn't teasing. This is just the beginning- oh God, yes, yes, just like that, you naughty girl. Oh God, just like that, that's perfect, that's- oh God, oh fuck, don't stop, I want to cum all over that pretty fucking face- oh shit! Yes! I'm cumming, I'm cumming!" She threw her head back, her eyes closed against the orgasm that seized her, thrashing and bucking with the waves of sensation sweeping through her while her features were consumed by that tranquil, almost far away look Richard knew all too well.

The orgasm seemed to go on and on in one long continuous wave, but was actually a series of smaller intense ones that crashed over just as the last was fading away. When it all became too much and her body crumpled, collapsing to the sheets on her hands and knees, her hips bucking against the girl's mouth. Yet with the girl's arms coiled around her thighs, even then she couldn't escape and she had to push the girl's mouth away.

It was the sexiest thing Richard had ever seen.

As outwardly sensual as his wife was, she looked almost angelic when she came. Watching her cum had always been one of his favourite parts of their sexlife. Yet watching her do so for someone else was like seeing it for the first time, and it was just as exciting.

"Mmmm… you greedy girl" Alice purred, blinking through the black spots fogging her vision and crawling back around to kneel beside Rebecca.

"I'm sorry, but Mrs Martin, your pussy tastes so good," Rebecca explained with a smile that was sweet and innocent despite the wetness that glistened on and around her lips.

Alice made a face of mock astonishment. "Oh, you naughty girl, I'm going to have to punish you for that." Lowering her head, she pressed her lips to Rebecca's in a slow kiss, deep and sensual, drinking her in with lush licks while reaching down her body to the heat pulsing between her legs.

"Mmm… please do."

"I bet you can't wait for it, can you?" Alice softly stroked a finger through her swollen folds before pushing it inside, all the way to the knuckle. Rebecca gasped at the stimulation, her body squeezing Alice's digit tightly.

Alice loved her responsiveness. "Want me to use this pussy again, you dirty girl? Such a tight, naughty little pussy. How did my husband ever fit his big dick in there?"

"I can take a lot more than you think." Rebecca got out. She was trying to sound confident, but Alice could feel the tension amassing inside her, betraying her closeness.

"Well, I guess we better see about that," she teased, withdrawing her finger and coolly looking across the room to where Richard sat.

"Come here, *Dick*."

Chapter Seven

The low purr of his wife's summons sent a delicious shiver of pleasure rippling straight down to Richard's cock. Dutifully, he pushed up from the chair and, doing his best to ignore his aching cock, walked to the bed, his legs unsure if they were stiff or shaky. Rebecca and Alice watched his every move, their eyes dark and hungry, their lush bodies entwined and ready to pounce like a pair of tigresses watching a clueless monkey walk into their trap.

"That's it..." Alice cooed, trailing a finger through Rebecca's folds, coating the digit in her cream, then raising it up to her mouth to suck it clean with a moan. "Mmm... you've been such a naughty boy, *Dick*. Keeping this tasty little pussy all to yourself. So now you're going to do the right thing and show me everything you two did behind my back."

"Everything?" He asked, his mouth dry as his thoughts swam with the idea of what she was proposing.

"Everything…" The slow curl of Alice's lips was pure wickedness. "I want to see you eat her creamy cunt… go balls deep and fuck her until she screams." Then she turned to Rebecca and, touching her glistening fingers to her chin, guided her to look her way. Holding her eyes, she purred, "and watch you wrap that sexy mouth around his big dick and suck him dry."

Rebecca blinked at the command. Scared and uncertain, she looked like she might refuse before all the desire that had gathered within her won out and she nodded.

"Good girl," Alice breathed, pressing a soft, almost chaste kiss to her mouth, but Richard didn't miss her lips parting ever so slightly. His wife moaned, a sound that doubled the ache in his imprisoned cock as she licked the last taste of herself from those soft lips. Rebecca moaned, her mouth opening under that gentle coaxing to suck greedily at the older woman's tongue as she took her hand and placed it on the bulge of his cock along his trouser leg. Together, they rubbed with fingers entwined, palms twisting and stroking up and down through the coarse material until someone snagged the clasp of his fly tail. They dragged it down while the other dealt with the button.

When it popped free and the vice around his cock eased, Richard couldn't help a sigh. It promptly became a groan, however, the moment his wife dragged the elastic of his boxers back and lodged them a little less than gently beneath his balls. Yet that sting was nothing compared to the feeling of long graceful fingers wrapping around him.

"Mmm… now put your mouth on his big cock…" Alice purred, pulling back just enough to watch, and angled the hard length of Richard's dick downward until the head, dark and swollen, hovered just over Rebecca's mouth.

The girl didn't hesitate. Leaning forward, she took his offered cock into her mouth. Her eyes peering up at him from beneath sex tussled hair as her lush pink lips slid over his crown. The lush heat of her mouth engulfing him in a single smooth glide, cheeks hollowing as she sucked.

Fuck.

It didn't matter that he'd cum twice already. If she carried on like this, he wouldn't last long.

"That's it… mmm… get it nice and wet," Alice teased, biting her lips as she watched Rebecca take him in as deep as she could before pulling back, leaving it wet and shiny. When just the wide crest remained, she reversed track, her hands coming up to brace against his thighs, giving her purchase to push her mouth back down, attacking his cock like she'd been starved of it, making up for whatever she lacked in skill with eagerness.

It was something Alice never thought she'd see. Something she never thought she'd want to. A taboo act of betrayal that she should have found repulsive, but instead was pushing all her hot buttons and made her tingling pussy throb.

Alice couldn't understand it. She was a proactive woman, not a voyeur. She didn't stand on side-lines. Where was the fun in just watching other people have sex? The very idea sounded no different from watching porn, without the deniability. Yet as she released her hold on Richard's cock to let Rebecca have her way with him, she wanted to watch.

This was so much more than pornography. Porn was manufactured, soulless, devoid of life and all the things that made sex so fun, little more than bodies going through the motions. Compared to that, this was art. Pure erotic art in the making, all induced to inflame the senses. The sounds of Rebecca's mouth as it slid along his cock, the way her eyes peered up at him with a knowing yet scared and pleading fashion. The way Richard's breathing changed as his hands fisted against the feeling it invoked in him, even as his body started circling, feeding her more of his cock. Even the heady scent of sex rolling from them to fog her brain had her panting. It was pure carnality. A drug she was powerless to resist.

"Suck it, yeah, that's it you dirty little slut, you like it don't you, you love sucking my husband's dick," she pressed, cupping her free hand over the deep throbbing between her legs, fingers massaging the knot of her clit. Not as roughly as she usually liked, but just enough to stoke the storm burning inside her.

Rebecca's eyes flickered back to Alice, almost sparkling with mischief as she pulled her mouth off their lover's cock. "Yes, but it's just so big. Can you show me how to suck it, Mrs Martin?"

"Oh, fuck…" Richard moaned, head spinning as something almost gave way inside him. It couldn't be helped. The vision of her kneeling there in all her naked beauty, a picture of angelic innocence with his cock still wet from her mouth, rising over her face as she said that. Well, it was almost enough to make him cum right there.

"Oh, you want to watch me?" His wife cooed back, all mock sweetness but for the sultry, wicked look that she fixed him with as she did. A look that always spelled trouble. Hot, sexy, fucking trouble.

Rebecca nodded, raising one hand to follow the line of veins that roped his cock. "Yes, please, teach me how to suck your husband's cock, Mrs Martin, please."

Fuck.

Yep, no doubt about it. They were genuinely trying to kill him.

"Alright, you dirty girl," Alice purred, slinking over gracefully to press a feather soft kiss to the girl's lips before gripping his cock. "Mmm… first, go slow and tease him. Just focus on the head, worship it with your mouth and tongue…" To demonstrate, she did just that, bending down to circle her tongue around the flared crest before wrapping her lips around it and sucking greedily. Already so hard and thick, the heated flesh pulsed with each little flutter of her tongue, his desire flowing over her taste buds and straight down to the slick heat throbbing at her core.

"Oh fuck… A-Alice, no… wait… not so…" he moaned, his hands fisting against the urge to grab her hair, the tip of his cock suddenly tingling like it was about to burst.

Alice ignored his entreaty.

"Then lick his dick like it's the biggest, juiciest fucking lollypop you've ever seen." Releasing his tip to turn her head from side to side, dragging her tongue down his cock's flanks and underside to the root, never once losing contact. "Don't forget his balls... take them into your mouth and lick them all over- mmm," she moaned, her hum reverberating around his balls as she opened wide to lodge one against the roof of her mouth, her tongue stroking the underside, sent waves of lust crashing over him. Holding his gaze, she suckled one then the other, cradling them with her tongue and rolling them over and over before releasing both to lick back up his length. "When he's all nice and wet, worship him with your mouth, sucking like you want to get every drop of his cum..."

"Ah fuck..." Richard groaned, almost beyond speech as he watched his wife suck him deep into her mouth. The feeling of warmth flowing over his cock to draw him into a font of liquid heat almost made his knees give way and he couldn't help grabbing at her head, needing more.

"No Dick, no touching," she snarled, slapping his hands away before grabbing him with both hands and swallowing him. With her lips stretched tight around his girth and cheeks hollowed, she slid her mouth up and down, smooth and steady, taking him as deep as she could on every swing. Forgetting everything else. Her every thought and focus was consumed with the taste of his flesh on her tongue. The feeling of his cock moving through her lips and swelling in her mouth. The tortured ecstasy on his face as he watched her and the feel of his body, taut and straining against itself in the race to orgasm.

These were the moments she lived for. To have so much power over one so big and strong, to drive them crazy with lust, it was more than any mere aphrodisiac. It was enough to make her fucking cum.

"Mrs Martin?" The softly spoken question brought her back to reality with a hot spike that went straight to her clit. She glanced up to see Rebecca watching in awe. Her once innocent doe eyes were dark with lust and her lush mouth opened and closed in quick, panting moans as one hand clutched at her breast, roughly tugging and twisting the nipple. The other was nestled between her legs and was working savagely at her clit.

Guess she likes to watch too.

A fresh rush of heat surged down to her core at the thought of the girl masturbating to a show of her sucking off her husband.

Pulling off, Alice smirked up at Rebecca and slowly licked the taste of her husband from her lips. "Mmm… such a big, yummy cock. He's easily big enough for two mouths. It needs two mouths…" She angled his cock towards her. "Come here."

It was an order that could not be disobeyed. Clearly knowing just what was expected, Rebecca swooped down and dragged the flat of her tongue up his shaft. From where Alice still gripped, up to the tip and the older woman's waiting mouth.

"Oh… Jesus… fuck…" Richard bit out, his words a tangled garble of grunts and moans as their mouths came together around him in an opened mouth kiss.

Already fighting his own building orgasm, he knew he should look away. Should close his eyes or cover them or… something. Anything. Anything to block out the sight of their tongues duelling around his tip, licking and lashing in that erotic battle for dominance that made his heart pound, but he couldn't.

The sight of them together, his wife and mistress, working together to drive him out of his mind. It was just so taboo, so erotic, so fucking hot, that he couldn't bear to look away.

Seeing the tormented ecstasy on her husband's face, Alice took pity on him and pushed his cock up into Rebecca's mouth.

"That's it, good girl, now suck my husband's dick like I showed you…" she instructed, releasing her grip on his cock so she could slide her tongue down the side, tracing the veins that bulged along its length. All the while watching as the girl picked up right where she'd left off, mouthing and sucking at his crown like she was trying to suck every drop of cum out of his balls. "Yes, just like that… I love watching you suck his cock, go on, show us what a good little cock sucker you are…" Her encouragement drew a ragged sound from her husband, and she glanced up to see he was still watching them. His eyes locked to the sight of the girl's mouth wrapped around over his cock. "Does that feel good, Dick? Haven't I made her into such a good little cock whore for you?"

"Yes… oh fuck, so good" he growled out, his voice harsh and guttural and despite herself, Alice felt that knot of jealously in her heart winding tighter.

It was the first time she had ever heard her man sound so desperate. So wild and untamed, and despite herself, that small little voice inside didn't like it. Didn't like that it was this girl's mouth bringing it out of him instead of hers. In all their time together, no matter all the little tricks and games she'd played, she'd never been able to break his reserve. She could arouse the animal in him, but it was still a chained beast all the same.

Alice wanted to be the one to do this to him, to arouse such passion, to break his chains and take him over the edge.

And there was only one way she was going to do that.

She didn't give Rebecca any warning. Drawing back, she raised a hand up to the back of Rebecca's head and pushed down firmly, forcing the girl's mouth down onto Richard's cock. She didn't resist, absorbed in the moment, she went with it, swallowing through the initial shock to take him all the way to the root as Alice came up, curled her free arm around his neck and crushed their mouths together in a hungry kiss.

And she knew, in that moment, for him, it was her mouth around his cock, deep throating him.

It was too much.

The intensity of his wife's kiss, along with the feeling of her soft, sensuous body pressed up against his as the lush heat wrapped around his cock sucked it in all the way, finally drove Richard over the edge. His hands fisted in the waves of soft hair, holding Rebecca right where she was as his hips circled up into her mouth, the instinctive urge to thrust and fuck too powerful to deny. Near molten heat surged up through his shaft, but Alice swallowed the incoherent sounds that flowed from him as thick and hot as the cum he was pumping down Rebecca's throat. She swallowed it all greedily, moaning with a sweet purr of satisfaction that coursed straight down to the base of his spine, adding to the waves of ecstasy.

Then the storm passed and it was as if every muscle in his body had turned to jelly. With spots dancing before his eyes, he stumbled, almost losing his balance as his knees gave with that sent him tumbling into the bed's warm embrace. Darkness clawed at the corners of his eyes and with his heart still pounding like a drum, sleep didn't exactly sound like a bad idea.

Alice, however, had no intention of letting him off so easily.

"Oh Dick…" she murmured, throwing one lushly smooth leg across to straddle him. A small smile playing across her lips as she gazed down at him, dark eyes burning with predatory hunger.

"Wow… it's still so hard." Rebecca voiced as she rolled over and almost straight into his cock, still hard and not showing any signing of shrinking. She let out a long admiring breath and the feel of it wafting across his over sensitive glans made him gasp.

She looked up at Alice. Those big doe eyes, once so sweet and innocent, burned with the same dark, lustful fire that met them. Her tongue slowly swept across her lips. "Thank you for sharing your husband's cock with me, Mrs Martin."

The sweet, almost innocent way the girl said the dirty words, like it was for giving her an extra cookie, sent a fresh shiver of arousal through her. "She's such a good girl, isn't she, Dick? So sexy and polite, and such a good little cock sucker..." In truth, Alice couldn't help being rather impressed. Good as she was, Richard was just too big for her to swallow whole, but Rebecca had taken to it like a natural. And she looked so sexy with her husband's cock in her mouth.

"Yes, so good," Richard groaned, his voice low and tortured as memories of Rebecca's mouth gliding along his cock swam before his mind's eye. Recollections that caused his dick to twitch eagerly.

Fucking treacherous bastard!

Alice cooed a sympathetic sound that did not meet the wicked glint in her eyes. "Now you stay right there, honey, there's something you need to see..." she told Rebecca while turning back to the view of her husband stretched out beneath her. The sight of his hard body still covered by his shirt and trousers, though they were open around his most impressive of attributes, made her arch a brow.

Those would have to go. It was time to reaffirm her claim.

"I can't wait to watch you fuck her." She leaned down to nip and lick at his jaw and neck, running her hands down his chest through his shirt, fingering the buttons open as they went. "I know I said I wanted to watch you eat her tasty little pussy next, Dick, but watching her suck your cock got me so hot, I just can't wait. Dick, I need to get fucked, and I want her to watch it. I want her to see us and know that you're mine." When the last button came loose and the shirt fell open above his already splayed trousers to reveal his taut abdomen and well-defined lines she loved to lick. Not exactly a six-pack, but age, with the help of a good diet and a healthy workout routine, had been kind to her husband.

She rolled her hips, stroking her creamy sex with his length. "You're mine, Richard."

"Yes," he hissed, his jaw tight as her fingers curled around him. Her touch was warm, her hand small but strong, and skilful squeezing returned him to full hardness with a groan. "Yours, and you're mine."

The promise in those words sent a rush of relief flooding through her. The dedication that no one would ever come between them, so familiar yet suddenly so new and important, was as true now as the day he'd first promised her. She could see it in his eyes, the look of savage devotion blazing within them as he watched her notch his wide crest against her cleft, coating it in her flowing cream. More acute than ever before. A fierce promise just for her that made her heart flutter, and core throb with an ache to feel him deep inside her.

"I love you-ohh!" The words left her in a rush, her stormy eyes widening with the feeling of his cock pushing inside her as she let her body drop.

Fuck, she never tired of that burn. The feeling of being stretched, filled, split in half.

"Oh Fuck… no… wait…" Richard groaned, hands grabbing for the lush fullness of her bum, trying to stop her as her inner tissues wrapped around him, squeezing and sucking greedily, trying to draw him deeper. His cock, despite all the day's prior orgasms having leached away much of his sense of feeling, was still over sensitive from the one Rebecca's mouth had sucked from him.

However, his wife was in no mood to listen.

Needing to have him, all of him, inside her, Alice pressed on regardless. Her hands moving to his shoulders, pushing against his restraining hold, nails biting into his flesh as inch after delicious inch filled her pussy, still so sensitive and tender from the night's bounty of orgasms.

"Alice…" he bit out through gritted teeth, his words threaded with pained ecstasy, and shutting his eyes against the delicious sensation. His every sense and reason focusing on their union as lush, velvety warmth enveloped him to the hilt, squeezing like a fist.

"No! Don't… don't you dare close your eyes." She breathed through the sensations, needing to see. Nothing thrilled her like watching him, seeing him so on edge. Looking into his eyes, feeling his cock throb and swell inside her, and letting him see what he was doing to her in turn, the wildfire about to consume her as he reached places so deep inside.

The intimacy was so searingly intense, it was as if they were the only two people in existence. Only when he obeyed and their eyes locked did she move.

She started slowly, with small rolls of her hips.

She always needed to start off slow. No matter how turned on or wet she got, he was just so big, and her body loved it.

"Oh! Oh God… oh fuck, yes, Dick, fuck!" Alice panted, almost losing herself in the feeling of his cock invading her. Reaching so deep inside. Touching all the places she'd never known existed before him. She could feel her inner tissues clenching around his thick cock, refusing to let him go as she circled her hips, making her feel every delicious inch of him.

"Oh fuck, Alice, shit, you feel so good. Ride me baby, ride my fucking dick…" he panted, his breathing almost ragged from the feeling of her cunt tightening around him. Her slick inner walls fluttered with a frenzy as Richard let her have her way with him, wanting nothing so much as to watch her, his wife, ride him to her climax.

The sight of his wife above him, riding him. The thick waves of her silky dark main bouncing in a wild, sexy mess. Her skin flushed from pleasure and shiny with misted perspiration he longed to lick. Her eyes blazing down at him, fierce and hungry. She looked so wild and beautiful. A goddess of sex and beauty, riding him triumphantly, glorious and all conquering.

"That's right, that's how you like it, right Dick?" She panted, her orgasm building fast and strong with each circle of her hips and the grind of her clit against the flat of his groin. Then, leaning down, flattening her bare breasts against his chest so her stiff nipples dragged over his flesh in a tease of friction, she attacked his neck with hungry sucking kisses, drinking in the salt of his skin. "Mmm… Isn't your wife's tight little pussy just the best?"

"Yes, fuck, the best, always the best- oh fuck!" he groaned, teeth gritted and arching his head back. Giving her greedy mouth free rein to lick across his skin, even as it all became too much. He needed to have her, his wife.

He needed to fuck her as much as she did him. Suddenly, his body was moving, churning up into her sultry rhythm. Drawing back as she rose, then thrusting up to meet her as she came back down, meeting her with wet slapping thrusts that had them both curling in ecstasy.

"Oh! Oh my god… oh fuck… yes, that's it, pound that pussy, pound your wife's naughty little pussy…"Alice moaned, her breath hot and ragged on his skin. Her blood boiling with lust, and burning from the urge to fuck, she bit and licked across his shoulder and neck. Up to suck on his earlobe before claiming his mouth to drive her tongue into his warmth, mimicking the motions of his cock thrusting up into the clinging silken warmth as his hands brought her crashing down to meet him.

Fuck, he was so strong when he got like this, so powerful and wild. She loved it. The feeling of every inch of his masculinity piercing her, filling her to the brim. His white knuckled grip on her hips, almost painful but so good, both steadying her and raising her up, then slamming her down. Driving her wild as they went faster and faster until she was almost bouncing on him, clawing at his body, her nails dragging trails of fire across his flesh as each plunge and thrust found all the sweet spots and sent her soaring to new heights.

Overwhelmed, she reared back, her spine curling in a song of pleasure as her release swept over her like a tidal wave. The sensations hit fast and hard, sweeping her into the starry abyss.

"Yeah, cum for me, babe…" he groaned, mesmerised by the vision of her riding him over the edge, the feel of her cunt wrapping around him, refusing to let go even as he kept up his assault with the instinctual drive to join her in release. To come together, but, fuck, it wasn't enough. His cock was rock hard, but even the sight of his wife's perfect tits bouncing with the feeling of her lush pussy clamping down and sucking him deep wasn't enough to take him over the edge. Nowhere near enough.

"Oh god! Fuck! Yes, yes, give me all that dick…. I need it… I love it… I… I…"Alice moaned out, riding her release hard. Her whole body shivering as he fucked her through the waves crashing over her, and streams of stars blasting across her vision. It was one of the most intense orgasms of her life, a carnal nuclear blast, and it would have been so easy for her to give in and let the feelings carry her away. But she couldn't. She wouldn't. Richard hadn't cum yet. She needed to make him cum. Needed to claim his last release and wash all this away.

And that was when she glimpsed Rebecca perched across from them on the other side of their wide queen-size bed. Her eyes wide with their deceptive innocence, even as one hand kneaded a breast, fingers tugging and twisting the nipple, while the other rubbed herself between her legs, circling over her clit.

Their eyes met amidst the orgasmic haze and Alice knew it was time to kick things up a gear. "I want to see you sit on his face, my little slut."

Richard almost couldn't believe his own ears. Fuck, had Alice really just say that?

Just the thought of his wife telling another woman to sit on his face sent a hot thrill down to the base of his spine that at any other time could have made him cum. Then Rebecca was kneeling over him and the question was suddenly academic as she gazed down at him, biting her lower lip. Her eyes uncertain behind the dark fog of lust.

It reminded him of how she had looked spread out beneath him that night in her room, scared but eager. Innocent yet naughty, his sweet temptation. He gave a nod, and releasing his grip on Alice, giving her the freedom to ride his cock, raised his hands up to cup Rebecca's buttocks, steadying her as she swung one lusciously long leg across his shoulders. Then, facing his wife, she slowly lowered her pussy down towards his mouth, flooding his senses with the thick heady musk of her arousal.

"Oh! Oh fuck… Mr Martin!" Rebecca moaned, throwing her head back in a long moan as Richard's lips enveloped her, his checks hollowing as he sucked hard on her clit. Her flavour flowed over his tongue, rich and thick as honey, and just as sweet as he remembered.

"Yeah, you like that, my little slut?" Alice asked, entranced by the sight of his jaw working, his tongue working with the fluttering licks she knew so well. Fuck, when had she become such a voyeur? Just watching him tease the small pearl of the girl's clit got her own bundle of nerves throbbing. Her walls flexing around him, the aftershocks of her previous release still tingling through her as she remembered the feeling of that very tongue dancing across her clit, so it was almost like she was getting fucked and licked all at once.

Just the thought of it almost made her lose her mind. Needing more, she ground and rolled her hips into his, angling her hips just right so his broad crest rubbed against a sweet spot. "Mmm… feels so good, doesn't it? Sitting on my husband's face? His mouth eating your pussy while I ride him…"

"Yes, oh fuck, so… good… oh yes! Right there, right there!" It was only half an answer, clearly too distracted by the lashing of Richard's tongue, but Alice didn't care. She was just so beautiful like that, caught up in the throes of passion. So wild and passionate, a complete contrast to usual bookish innocence. It made her ache to taste her again and cupping the girl's face in her hands, she pulled her in to claim her mouth in a kiss. Thrusting her tongue into her sweetness to feast on her sweetness, drinking her in the way her husband was doing to her cunt.

Denied any sort of visual but hearing and picturing everything, it was all Richard could do to ignore the way his wife slid along his dick, bearing down on him like a silken glove. Rather, he focused all his attention on making Rebecca cum. Greedy to taste her orgasm, he curled his arms around her hips, digging his fingers into her buttocks and crushing her against his mouth and sucking at her clit.

"Oh god!" Rebecca gasped, dragging her mouth from Alice's and throwing her head back.

Needing more, Alice shifted, leaning in to suckle on the girl's neck as she rocked her hips, her next orgasm building hard and fast. "He's got such a good mouth, but his cock's even better…" she purred in her ear, catching the lobe between her teeth and biting playfully. "Such a big fucking dick, so hard and thick, feels so good…"

"Yes. Yes. Yes!" The words were out in such a rush, whether they were in agreement or a vocalisation of her pleasure, it was hard to tell.

Regardless, the result was the same.

"Do you want to feel it, feel his big cock stretch out your tight little hole… fucking you so deep… making you take every fucking inch…" Alice pressed, trailing kisses down the girl's neck.

"Oh god, please…" Rebecca whimpered, arching up into the other woman's touch, clawing Richard's chest for any sort of purchase.

Richard felt how the dirty talk was affecting not just Rebecca, but Alice too, making him groan into the girl's folds as his wife's clamped down on him, her walls squeezing him tight. His body answered without his volition, bucking and screwing his cock up into her luscious pussy.

"Please what, my little slut?" Alice asked, teetering right on the edge but wanting to watch Rebecca cum one more time. Heat rushed over her with the feeling of his cock moving inside her as she watched that sweet face contort so beautifully with pleasure. She bent down and caught a lush nipple between her lips. Sucking once before swirling her tongue around and around, then switching to the other. "Do you want me to let my husband fuck you? Go on, tell me how badly you want to feel his big cock filling up your tight little cu-"

"Yes! Oh fuck, please, please Mrs Martin, please can I fuck your husband… ohhh god… mmm… I can't wait, I need to feel his dick inside me. Please, let me fuck it, I want to fuck your husband's cock, I need it, I… I… oh fuck!"

Richard felt Rebecca's release break as he swirled his tongue around her inner walls, her thighs snapping closed around his head, squeezing so tight he could barely breathe amidst the smooth, warm flesh as she bucked and ground against his tongue. Regardless, he licked her through it, greedily drinking her in, lapping up every drop of her cream, the taste of her gilding his cock to steel.

Alice felt it too, the sudden surge of his arousal swelling inside her as Rebecca's body trembled and shook against hers. And she watched, avidly, needing to see that look in those big eyes one more time. See the pleasure, the releases, the freedom, the complete carnal abandon all billowing together in a perfect storm within those innocent doe eyes.

See it, remember it, and know that *they* had done this to her.

Just the thought of it shattered her mind into shards that cascaded across the heavens with each fresh pulse of white hot pleasure. Consumed by sheer sensation, she claimed Rebecca's lips in a desperate kiss, hugging her close as their bodies quaked together, clinging to her for dear life until the storm passed. Then the world moved, and they were crashing back down to earth, landing with a soft bounce upon the bed.

Richard didn't hesitate. Almost mindless with the need to fuck, to cum, to bury his cock inside them both and brand them both with his seed. One quick twist was all it took to send both of them tumbling off him to the covers. Then he was up, shrugging out of his shirt and kicking off his trousers, before rolling up onto his knees.

Rebecca's soft round bum wiggled enticingly as he came up behind her and, grabbing her waist with both hands, he rolled her over onto her hands and knees and dragged her back towards him. Still slick with his wife's cream, his cock plunged in deep, going all the way to the root with his first thrust.

"Oh my… Oh fuck! Yes, yes!" Rebecca gasped, looking back over her shoulder at him. Her eyes hot and lusty, calling out to him with a lustful passion in an unabashed plea for him to take her, dominate her, fuck her.

With a low growl, he began to move. Pulling back almost enough to slip free, before driving back home so his abdomen slapped against her checks with a wet smack as she pushed back.

"That's a good girl, mmm… take that big dick… that's it, take it, let him in…" Alice purred, her lip caught provocatively between her teeth and eyes smouldering as she watched them rut. Drinking in the sight of him, so big and strong, using her like a little bitch in heat and dominating her so completely as he drove in with a reckless abandon, like she was nothing but a hole to be used for his pleasure. And Rebecca was clearly loving it, her eyes almost rolling in ecstasy. Not that Alice could blame her, knowing how good it felt to have that cock filling her up. That he felt even bigger from behind and could reach even deeper. "Let your little pussy take it. That's a good girl, such a good little slut. Let him have you. Tell him how good it feels… how big and deep my husband's dick is…"

Stretched out as she was, she lay alongside them with her head propped on one hand and one leg bent at an angle for them to glimpse the fingers of the other reaching down between her legs.

Just like that, Richard was right on the edge.

The vision of his wife spreading her legs open further, revealing the slick and swollen state of her well fucked pussy as her fingers circled her clit, almost pushing him almost past his limit. While this wasn't the first time he'd seen her masturbate, he knew he would never tire of watching her. She was such a sexual woman, unceasingly sensual and a complete agent provocateur. He dared the universe to create a more awe-inspiring sight than that of Alice pleasuring herself.

"So-so big… so deep… Oh my god… oh my god… right there, holy shit, Mr Martin, you feel so fucking good!" Rebecca gasped, mewling like a kitten as her hips rocked, greedy for more, her back curling as she pushed back, straining to take him deeper. The waves of untamed hair spilling down over her shoulders and across the bed as she bowed with the pleasure of it. Head down and arse raised, accepting his cock and the pounding it was giving, her moans muffled a bit by the sheets as she buried her head in them, even biting down against high sobs. Hands fisting and twisting and knotting the sheets as he fucked her. Harder. Faster. Needing to feel her cum just one more time.

"Naughty girl, you really wanted my cock, didn't you?" he husked, his voice low and guttural, thick with a primal edge, the beast in him taking over. "Fuck… such a snug little cunt…" he groaned, loving the view of his cock sliding through her folds, smooth as silk, then reappear slick with her cream. The pretty pink of her pussy stretched wide and her butt rippled with each meeting while his balls swung up to slap her clit.

"Yes, yes, fuck, please, please make me cum, make cum all over your- oh shit, fuck, fuck!" Her pleas were raw and desperate, rising high to the heavens and merging with the echoing *slap, slap, slap* of their meeting bodies. With each draw and thrust, fresh proof of her arousal rolled down his thighs.

"That's it, it feels so good having all of his big dick inside you, doesn't it?" Alice coaxed, her eyes lingering on the sight of Rebecca's breasts, full and firm, swaying with the movements of her body. Her fingers quickened, as if she was trying to match their pace, the tense, throbbing heat in her core spreading outward, spiralling through to her fingers and swollen nipples. "Yeah, I know how good it feels, but you mustn't be selfish…" And just to prove her point, she lent up to catch the nipple of one swaying breast between her swollen ruby lips, sucking gently before spinning away and shimmying around until she was sat up with both legs on either side of Rebecca's head "Now, are you going to be a good little slut and eat my pussy while you get fucked by my husb- oh!"

From his angle, Richard could just glimpse over her shoulder to see Rebecca pressing her face between his wife's legs. Though he couldn't quite see what she was doing, the wet sounds of her tongue were more than enough for his imagination to fill in the blanks.

Alice had no such obstacles.

With her heart thumping as the sexual energy sizzled through her blood, she couldn't bear to look away. Even as her head rolled back into the sex rumpled sheets, she was hooked. Captivated by the image of Rebecca's face between her legs, those beautiful eyes staring up at her from beneath a wing of dark hair while that tongue fluttered over her folds.

It was such an erotic view, one that put her right on the edge as she rimmed her hole, drinking her in. "Oh… Oh fuck… Oh my god… yes that's it, right there… oh fuck… look at you… eating my pussy… you're so sexy… so perfect… so fucking go- oh god, oh god, oh god…" Fireworks burst behind her eyes when the girl's mouth suddenly reacquainted itself with her clit. "Yeah, that's it, that's the spot, yes, good girl, you love that yummy pussy, don't you?"

"Oh fuck, yes, Miss Martin… fuck, I love it… so-so good, more… please… give me more…" She whimpered back, her answer smothered against her folds, but thick with desire and rising high as Richard filled her with his cock, pounding her and deep. Yet her eyes always stared up at her, gaze fixed upon her face and lips shiny with her cream as she sucked and licked.

It was all too much, but nowhere near enough, and each little pull of suction had her fisting Rebecca's silky hair and forcing her mouth harder against her cunt. "Fine Slut, you'll have more." Alice panted, her body burning. Her core was hot and throbbing and unbearably slick from the feeling of that tongue swirling around her clit. "Yes, eat that pussy, my little slut, eat my pussy and make me cum all over that pretty face."

The pleasure in her voice was a plea Richard knew all to all too well, a desperate instinctual sound, wild and primal. A sound only he had reduced her to.

He couldn't stand it.

With a growl, he started sliding Rebecca back and forth, fucking her cunt onto his cock in time to meet his pounding thrusts. Driving into her harder, deeper, until his broad crest was banging against the gates of her core. Even then, he couldn't get deep enough, the primal beast in him needing to both claim and punish this little minx.

Alice felt the change in him. Felt it in the sudden jarring thrusts that had Rebecca's mouth and tongue grinding over her pussy, and the moans that reverberated around her clit shot through her like white hot electricity, nearly making her cum every time he went balls deep. Then hands were grabbing onto her and crushing her sex to Rebecca's mouth as the suction around her bundle of nerves grew stronger and more desperate, like the girl was trying to suck in air through her pussy.

"Yes! That's it… yeah, so fucking good… yes…" she moaned, her eyes flickering up to his, recognising the look that burned back at her. Saw how good he felt, how close he was. She loved it. She loved watching him lose it and tilting her head back, she fixed him with a look that was pure wickedness. "Fuck her, Dick!" One hand clutching at her breasts, fingers twisting and tugging at the coral tips to ease the ache inside. The other fisted the waves of Rebecca's hair and pressed her face hard to her pussy as the girl's cheeks hollowed with a suction that had her bucking up off the bed. "Fuck her and make her cum! Make her cum all over your cock!"

"Oh fuck, Alice... don't... stop talking like that..." Richard barked, his breath seething through gritted teeth at the feeling of Rebecca's inner tissues squeezing him. Growing tighter with his wife's every word, tight and hot and wonderfully snug, trying to hold him in, refusing to let go. It felt good, too fucking good.

Alice's eyes flash at his outburst, her heart thumping and rolling and twisting a peaked nipple close to the point of sweet agony. "Oh, does my little slut like it when I talk dirty?"

"Oh yeah, she loves it..." And as he said it, punctuating each word with the slap of flesh on flesh, Rebecca moaned helplessly, her body shaking with the orgasm ripping through her.

However, Alice ignored him, her eyes fixed upon the eyes peering up at her from between her legs.

"You like getting fucked like the little bitch in heat you are, don't you?" She pressed, tightening and twisting her hold on her hair while her hips rocked and ground against her tongue, straining up into the lush heat. Her core was tight and throbbing and eager to cum again. "Look at you, eating my pussy while getting fucked. That's my husband's dick inside you, filling up your pussy, my little slut. Yes, suck my clit while you take his big cock. That's right, make me cum on your face while you take my husband's big fucking cock..."

"Do you like watching your husband fuck me, Mrs Martin?" Rebecca asked, raising her head slightly to ever so softly tongue her bundle of nerves with soft flicks. Yet beneath her pleasure flushed face, her eyes were pleading and desperate, needing to hear it. As if deep down, she still harboured doubts.

"Oh sweetie… I love it, watching you take my husband's cock while eating my pussy is so fucking sexy- oh fuck… oh fuck!." Alice's whole body bucked, an orgasm crashing over her when Rebecca's mouth enveloped her, that wicked little tongue thrusting deep to swirl inside her. It was like she was trying to find and lick all her sweet spots at once, sending fresh waves rippling through her, pushing her release on and on, until black dots were dancing before her eyes.

She couldn't bear it. It was too much. She was too sensitive, and with a last gasp, she pushed her head away. "Enough…"

Richard watched his wife succumb to her orgasm with his own not far behind. The sight of it almost pushed him over the edge, yet he wanted more and stubbornly tried to hold it at bay. His eyes rolling back up to the ceiling, trying to focus on something, anything, to distract him. Distract him from the feeling of Rebecca's lush walls, milking him with greedy pulses. From the sight of his wife writhing in such sweet oblivion, and his cock sliding through the swells of the girl's butt, disappearing inside her sweet cunt.

Seeming to know his mind, Alice, with the spots fading but her body still tingling, lurched up to kiss his mouth. "And you Dick…" she husked, kissing like she owned him. Needing him to know he was here, and she was his. Her hands rubbing their way up the tense muscles of his arms and shoulders to fist the rough brush of his hair, crushing his mouth to hers. "Did you enjoy watching our little slut eat me while you fuck her?" A deep, guttural growl rose in him to answer her, sending shivers of desire rushing up her spine. His control slipping, his hips snapped with harder, faster strokes that literally fucked Rebecca down into the bed beneath them. "Doesn't her naughty twenty-year-old cunt feel good wrapped around your big, hard cock?"

"Yes, fuck, shit, so fucking good…!" He groaned, shaking with the tensions threatening to overwhelm him. The heat of her words tingling down his spine to stir the telltale throbbing down in the base of his spine. "Ahh Shit! Fuck… I'm going to cum!"

"No, net yet Dick." She ordered, pulling back just far enough to flick the tip of her tongue teasingly over his nose, but the purpose burning in her eyes steeled him to obey and linger in that hellish purgatory. "Turn her over. Let's finish her together."

Near mad with his need to cum, Richard didn't question her. Without losing his rhythm, he tensed his grip and rolled Rebecca over onto her back. Rebecca squeaked at the sudden twist, but before she asked, Alice threw a leg over her body and leaned down, their bodies fitting together like puzzle pieces sliding into place, her eyes glued to where his cock was gliding through her folds.

"Mmm… that's it baby… Your dick looks so good going in and out of her pussy." Her mouth watering at the sight of the wetness that was coating his cock with each thrust, she leant in and swept her tongue through Rebecca's folds.

Richard couldn't believe his eyes. "Oh, fuck… Alice…"

She didn't answer. Relishing the heady taste of their mixed juices, she twisted her head ever so slightly to slide between their grinding bodies, licking ravenously, greedy for every drop. Unceasing even as beneath her, Rebecca wrapped her arms around her thighs and bent up to attack her clit, sucking with equal hunger. Swollen and so sensitive from too many orgasms so close together, the sudden rush of sensation was so intense, it was almost too much. But she fought on, suddenly needing both her lover and her husband to be there with her.

Richard already was, and certain he might lose his mind at any moment, he went with her. Blindly reaching down to grasp the back of Rebecca's legs, he pushed them back to frame Alice's shoulders, opening her fully and tilting her hips up towards her devouring tongue. The vision of his wife's head between Rebecca's legs, licking her clit as he fucked her, driving him wild. Past the point of no return, he pounded into the girl's lush grasping heat with his last reserves, going so rough, the bed shook, the headboard banging against the wall in a call that screamed hot, passionate sex to any that cared to be listening. He didn't care. He didn't care if the entire building, or everyone in the whole damn city knew what they were doing. All that mattered was them. He and Alice, together till the dawn, and whatever wonders lay beyond as they walked together, side by side and hand in hand, into this new chapter of their lives.

"That's it Dick, hold her legs back like that... mmm... so sexy... such a sexy little pussy... I love watching you fuck her... yeah... fuck that pussy..." Alice moaned, grinding down onto that wonderful mouth. The high rising moans that poured from her every time she watched Richard's cock driving into the root, reverberating around her clit and through her, out across her nerves, until she felt like a string too tightly plucked and about to snap. Her pussy was hot and throbbing, burning with need. She could sense it in Rebecca too, and met her husband's gaze, needing to see, to watch him go over that edge again. Her eyes were hot and daring him to deny her as she rolled Rebecca's clit with her tongue. "She's such a good little slut for us... yes... Now baby... fill her sweet little pussy up, Dick. I want to lick all your cum out of her... cum for me."

It was a command he was powerless to resist.

"Fuck, fuck, fuck!" he grunted as he pounded into the girl for the final time, burying himself to the root, white hot fire burning out from the base of spine. Stars raced across his eyes with each pulse of heat that shot through him and for a moment, it felt like he was caught in a vortex, having his soul sucked out of his body in the most powerful orgasm of his life. Every sensation was so intense, it was agony.

An exquisitely sweet agony, made all the more potent by Alice watching him.

Alice loved watching Richard cum. Hearing the ragged sounds as he dragged in breaths. Seeing the pleasure twisting and contorting his usually so calm expression, the wild look in his eyes. Feeling that shudder course through him as he flooded her cunt. There was nothing sexier than seeing her man climax, and knowing it was because of her. Even now, he was cumming, flooding Rebecca's pussy with his seed for her.

She couldn't bear it. Her own climax hit like a storm as Rebecca's orgasmic moans bombarded her clit. Fuelled by its passion, she pushed him back just in time for his cock to slide free and release the last spurt of his cum across her breasts. Before she took him into her mouth, lips stretching across his crown, cheeks hollowing.

"Oh shi... Alice!"

Moaning at the taste of pussy on his flesh, she sucked hard and didn't release his shrinking length until she'd cleaned it of every drop. Yet that wasn't enough to quench her thirst and even before Richard had tumbled back onto the bed, she'd buried her face back down between Rebecca's legs. Caught up in the trailing after glow of so many powerful orgasms much too close together, she could only tremble and moan as Alice lapped at the mingled juices, thrusting her tongue deep.

Only when she'd scooped up as much of her husband's cum as she could reach did she pull away and, turning around, crawled shakily up the girl's body. With the taste of them still on her tongue, she took her face in her hands and softly kissed her trembling lips, feeding her their mingled juices before cupping her cum-splashed breasts and raising them up for the girl clean.

"Good girl." She praised once the job was done, before pulling her close as she let herself finally give into the softness of the bed and the warm soft body beside her. Then the darkness at the edge of her vision consumed her.

Epilogue

"Where's Alex? I'm guessing you didn't do all this with him just down the hall." Richard mused, staring up at the darkened ceiling above. He hadn't needed to look to know Alice was awake. He just sensed it.

She was snuggled against his right side with an arm draped across his chest. On his left, Rebecca was still asleep, with her arms locked securely around his arm and her head on his shoulder. He didn't bother to wonder how they'd ended up like that. From being spiralled casually around the bed to snuggled together beneath the sheets with their heads just managing to fit together all on one pillow. In the grand scheme of things, that seemed rather inconsequentially irrelevant at this point.

His wife didn't look at him, nor even open her eyes as she snuggled closer, her head resting on the place between his shoulder and pectoral, the softness of her breasts pressed against his ribs. "Hmm... No, he's with my parents. I dropped him there this morning before work and said I'd pick him up on my way home in a couple of days."

"Thank god for that." He grinned, chuckling to himself. "Otherwise, by the time he hits puberty, we'd be spending all our money on shrinks."

That made the corner of Alice's mouth curl wryly as her fingers drew circles across her. "Well, don't count it out just yet. Poor boy, who knows what nightmares he might have after a couple of days staying with my parents... But mum's been nagging for some time with him, so I thought why not take advantage and have a little *quality time*."

It was impossible to miss her sultry purr, and the salacious meaning of it sent a hot shiver down his spine, reawakening his cock, though it complained bitterly at the sums. "oh, so um... how did this..." He glanced down at Rebecca, whose face was a mask of innocence and serenity, betraying none of the deeds she'd performed that day that were at such a stark contrast to anything anyone would call innocent.

Though she couldn't see with her eyes still closed, she understood his meaning. "Her dad thought she'd stolen something of his and got rough with her again."

He stiffened at her words, but the tension in him seemed to disturb the girl on his arm as she shifted suddenly. So he forced himself to relax.

"That bastard," He bit out.

There was so much fire and barely restrained venom in his voice that Alice opened her eyes. "Relax, I took care of it," she purred, leaning in to press soft kisses to his throat as the hand on his chest slid down the line of his abdomen.

"Yeah… how bad?" he asked, swallowing as he felt her hand working lowering, and his body responding to it. Her slow sucking kisses quickly smothering one fire with another. The tempting wench…

Edging higher, she took the lobe of his ear between her teeth and bit hard enough to make him hiss. "Mmm… let's just say he'll think twice before attacking a woman half his size again."

"He what!" He jerked back suddenly, his head snapping round to fix her with a look that was almost murderous. "Fucking hell, that's it! I'll kill him."

He meant it too. Alice could see the fury in his eyes, the murder. While Richard would never intentionally hurt her, she'd always known he could and would kill for her. Would do whatever it took to protect her and their son. She loved him for it, and at times it was a major turn on to see and feel him cut loose and go all alpha male.

But it wasn't helping now.

"No, you won't. It's done. I handled it, so forget it," she said, moving her hand back to his heaving chest, urging him back down to the bed. Besides them, Rebecca stirred, rolling away from them. That movement seemed to help ease his storm, and he nodded for her to continue. "Anyway, we came in. I ran her a bath. Then we got talking and…"

"Things came out," he offered quickly, voice heavy and eyes dropping low.

Shame twisted his guts into tight knots.

"Yeah, you could say that," she shrugged, trying to look nonchalant about it, but even as she said the words, she had to look away, unable to meet his eyes.

She still felt it still, that hurt, the sting of betrayal, his betrayal.

That he could have hurt her so cut him deeper than any blade. "I'm sorry, I don't know what came over me… it just sort of-"

She nodded. "*Happened*. Yeah, I know."

The coolness in her tone could have cut glass.

"But now you're okay with… everything." It was a stupid as fuck question to ask and he knew it as soon as he said it, but he needed to know. Needed to know if she could move past this.

"Well, I wouldn't exactly say I'm over the moon about you fucking our babysitter behind my back…" She let the words hang there for a moment, and time seemed to hold its breath before she met his eyes once again. "But then again, I'm not exactly in any position to judge, am I? We weren't exactly playing truth or dare and having a pillow fight when you burst in, now, we're we?"

And just like that, all the tension had suddenly vanished as she smiled up at him.

Despite himself, Richard couldn't help but grin back at her. "No, I guess not."

She nodded. "So, it's agreed then. Next time, we discuss things first, then we fuck them."

Her husky promise turned his cock to stone. "Next time?"

"Well, you enjoyed tonight, didn't you?" she asked, climbing atop his waist so the stiff, and still a little sore, head of his cock was notched against her folds. "No one said it has to stop. Where's the fun in having a bi-sexual wife if you can't experiment a bit?"

"Bi, huh? When did that start?" he arched his brow as his hands brushed down her spine to cup her buttocks, loving the feel of their firmness filling his hands. His wife really had the greatest ass, and though they'd never discussed doing anal, he couldn't help wondering if she'd be interested.

"It's new…" she purred, giving a slow roll of her hips that coated him in her quickening cream and teased her clit. "Something I'm thinking about trying. Care to help?"

"Sure, where's the harm in a bit of *experimentation*…" His hands squeezed her arse suggestively, grinding her harder against his shaft, one finger reaching out, wetting itself in her juices then teasing across her puckered anus, pressing just hard enough to make her gasp.

"Oh! You naughty boy! I'll remember you said that…" she teased while pushing back just enough to feel herself opening beneath the tip, but just the tip. "Maybe we should bring a boy to bed next time. I could suck all his cum out while you fuck me. Wouldn't that be fun?"

"Cheeky," he groaned and, pulling back, gave her ass a swat that had her gasping with a mix of surprise and pleasure. "I think I better give you a spanking for that one."

Alice's eyes lit up at the prospect. "Oh, please do-"

"Ummm… Mr & Mrs Martin?" A small voice cut in.

Stilling, they turned to see Rebecca staring back at them from her side of the pillow.

Alice smiled and reached out to stroke her check. "I think you can call us Richard and Alice now, honey."

However, the girl edged away from the touch, her big doe eyes glassy and lip quivering. "Sorry, it's just… Well, I'm sorry I've caused you both so much trouble. You've both been so kind to me, and I... well… Maybe I should go…" With crystal tears rolling down her cheeks, she threw back the sheets and jumped off the bed, the pale skin of her naked body almost seeming to glow in the low light.

Quick as a snake, Richard's hand shot to catch her arm and pulled the sobbing girl back down to the bed. "Hey, hey… shhh… it's alright…. You've never been any trouble for us."

"Yeah, it's all alright," soothed Alice, wrapping her arms around the girl and pulling her into a hug. "You're safe with us, besides I said you could stay with us while you figure out what you want to do, and so stay with us you shall."

Slowly, Rebecca raised her head to look at the couple, her eyes uncertain, as if she was too afraid to believe them. "Really… you don't mind… even after I…"

"Fucked my husband?" Alice shot her husband a sideways look, her tongue sweeping across her lips. "No, I rather enjoyed watching it, if I'm honest." Bending down, she kissed her tears away. "I don't mind sharing him with you, though I'm not sure I'm ready to share you with him yet. Maybe you should convince me…" She kissed her deeply, licking into her mouth, mimicking the same motions she'd used on her pussy until the girl softened and moaned beneath her. "The night is still young, and I think it's time I introduce you to a very special friend of mine." She rolled away, onto the other side of the bed, and opened her bedside table drawer. Seeing what she wanted, she grabbed it and rolled back to face the pair with a grin that was pure wickedness.

In her hand, she grasped a XL magic wand rechargeable vibrator.

"This is Antonio."

The End

A note from the Author

Thank you for reading the sweet Temptations Trilogy.
This is the end of the Trilogy but far from the end for Richard and
Alice. Over the years I've given great amounts of thought to their
respective stories and there is so much more left to tell. They still
have secrets waiting to be discovered. Their enemies will want their
revenge, and of course, there is the Rebecca situation to consider?
Can the three of them make it work, or was this just a Sweet
Temptation?
This is not the end, it's only the beginning of their adventures.

**To learn about my upcoming works and follow their upcoming
adventures, sign up to my newsletter via:**
https://www.subscribepage.com/w7y7k2
Subscribers receive a FREE book with every newsletter.

About The Author

L.M. Mountford's goal in life is to be unique, a character who stands out from the crowd that you just can't help remembering with a bemused chuckle.

A born and bred country boy from the southwest of England, he knew from an early age that he wanted to write and spent most of his time writing story ideas or playing Star Wars on his PlayStation.

Not much has changed over the years, though his stories have grown decidedly dirtier, and he swapped the Star Wars for Call of Duty.

Dubbed the Lord of Lust in 2019 and a firm believer that nothing sells like sex and violence, he loves writing about hard and gritty romantic thrillers, loaded with action men, sassy heroines, and a whole lot of dirty, sexy heat.

He also loves meeting and chatting with readers who love his work. You can connect with him on facebook, or subscribe to his newsletter for regular updates.

Learn more about him and follow his journey on Social Media here:
https://linktr.ee/lmmountford

Bibliography

For a complete reading list, visit LMMountford.com/bibliography/

Collections
Deliciously Sinful Liaisons
Sweet Temptations Box Set
Romancing the Tropics
Just a Number
Alpha Men of the Otherworld
Dirty Daddies
Rogue Warrior
Rogue
The Sweet Temptations Series
The Babysitter
The Boss's Daughter
Broken Heart Series
Broken
Tropical Cocktail Romance
Tequila Sunset
Beneath the Sheets
Confessions of a Trophy Wife
Forbidden Desire
Stand-alone Titles
Uncovered
Serving the Senator
Training Tracey

Also by L.M. Mountford

Age is just a number, and this collection of sinfully steamy age-gap romances will prove it…

The Lord of lust has done it again and in this anything but sweet, four book Box Set, full of forbidden Silver Foxes and sassy Cougars, he proves that age is no boundary to love, or lust.

A collection of hot and orgasmic stories by The Lord of Lust
Do you love hard men, strong women, sizzling chemistry and erotic
scenes that make Fifty Shades of Grey look like five shades of beige?
Well, here you go…
7 Books, 7 hard and rugged men, 7 sizzling page turners that will
have you devouring every word from start to finish…

Five years ago, I was the DeCampo Familia's most feared enforcer, then they killed me...

Now I'm in hiding, a dead man walking.

All I had to do was keep my head down, live a quiet, normal life.

But normal is a hard thing for a man like me.

I might just have been able to manage it, if trouble hadn't come looking for me

In the form of a feisty barmaid.

A vixen probably half my age, with long raven hair and a backside that promised all sorts of trouble.

Hot, sweaty, all night long sorts of trouble.

I should have stayed away, but I was hooked from the moment she sashayed through the doors of the bar.

And when a few of the patrons started getting rough with her, the old me was ready to give them a lesson in manners.

However, times have changed. I wasn't in New York anymore and getting into a bar fight with five guys for her honour wasn't the way to this girl's heart or into her pants.

Good thing I'm stubborn, because while her attitude might be frosty, the chemistry between us is hot and I'm not about to let her get away.

So first things first, I need to learn her name.

And just hope my past doesn't catch up with me
and kill me first...

A Tropical Cocktail Boxset
Romance is in the air in this two book Holiday Romance boxset that
is all about sun, sea and sex…
Tequila Sunset
Beneath The Sheets

Alpha Men of the Otherworld
The battle of the Species is about to rage, and only the true alpha
will come out on top in the Lord of Lust hottest new duo boxset that
sees vampires and werewolves lock tooth and claw…

THEIR SILENCE COMES AT A PRICE...

UNCOVERED

THE LORD OF LUST

L.M. MOUNTFORD

When Mina returns for her stepbrother's 21st birthday, she thinks her days of lusting after him are over. Caught up in the heat and passion of the moment, she is stunned to find them back in bed together; their feelings clearly far from resolved.

Haunted by her desire, Mina now has another problem... she must head down a path of lust and desire; torn between the dark delights of the handsome bad boy down the street and her adorable stepbrother who has always been there for her. Can she confront the truth she has long tried to bury? How far will she go to save the one she wants, but knows she can never truly have?

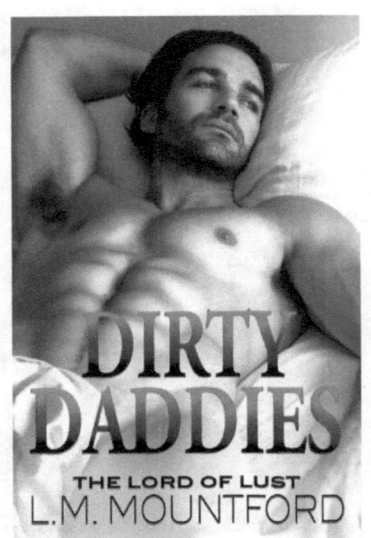

The Politician. The Billionaire. The Detective. Three hot alpha males.
Three steamy older men, younger woman age gap romances.
*The Dirty Daddies is a three book boxset from The Lord of Lust, holding
three of his hottest older man, younger woman steamy age gap romances.*